The People of the Pole

The People of the Pole

by
Charles Derennes

translated, annotated and introduced by
Brian Stableford

A Black Coat Press Book

Visit our website at www.blackcoatpress.com

ISBN 978-1-934543-39-9. First Printing. April 2008. Published by Black Coat Press, an imprint of Hollywood Com-
ics.com, LLC, P.O. Box 17270, Encino, CA 91416. All rights
reserved. Except for review purposes, no part of this book may
be reproduced or transmitted in any form or by any means,
electronic or mechanical, including photocopying, recording,
or by any information storage and retrieval system, without
permission in writing from the publisher. The stories and
characters depicted in this novel are entirely fictional. Printed
in the United States of America.

Introduction

Le peuple du Pôle, here translated as "The People of the Pole," was originally published in 1907; it was one element of a "new wave" of French scientific romance, which avidly absorbed the recent influence of the English writer H. G. Wells into the solid but slightly tired tradition launched 40 years earlier by Jules Verne. Its author, Charles Derennes, was then in his mid-20s—he had been born in 1882—and *Le peuple du Pôle* was his second novel, following *L'amour fessé* [approximately and somewhat euphemistically translatable as "Bruised Love"], which had been published the previous year. His father, Gustave Derennes (1858-1889), had also been a writer of some repute, although he is only remembered today for an early tourist guide to the French Alps and a series of eulogistic essays collected as *Les coeurs héroïques* [Heroic Hearts].

Like most ambitious writers of the period, the younger Derennes had begun his career writing poetry and critical essays for the periodicals that abounded at the time, including the *Mercure de France,* which had been co-founded by Alfred Vallette and Rémy de Gourmont as a flagship of the Symbolist *avant-garde. Le peuple du Pôle* was issued under the *Mercure*'s imprint, thus taking its place in a stratum of the literary marketplace some way above the one occupied by such near-contemporary Wells-influenced works as Arnould Galopin's *Le docteur Oméga* (1906; tr. in a Black Coat Press edition as *Doctor Omega*) and Gustave Le Rouge's *Le prisonnier de la planète Mars* (1908; tr. with its sequel in the Black Coat Press volume *The Vampires of Mars*). While those more downmarket works transplanted Wellsian themes and methods into an action/adventure framework similar to the one that became a staple of the US pulp magazines, Derennes remained loyal to the more ambitious tradition of satirical *contes philosophiques* whose sciencefictional strand extended all the way back to Voltaire's classic *Micromégas* (1752).

H. G. Wells saw himself as a formulator of *contes philosophiques* rather than a writer of action/adventure stories, although his early works certainly gave his readers abundant opportunity to misconstrue his intentions, and would certainly have found *Le peuple du Pôle* much more to his taste than Galopin's and Le Rouge's cavalier Martian fantasies. It seems probable that his influence, in this particular instance, was filtered through a fictionalized philosophical study published two years before *Le peuple du Pôle* by Anatole France, *Sur la Pierre blanche*, whose title is echoed in the title of Chapter VI of the novel's carefully-framed narrative, *"Sur la pierre brune."* France's book takes the form of a modernized classical dialogue analyzing the hazards of attempting to anticipate the future, punctuated by two exemplary novellas. One of the participants in the dialogue complains that futuristic visionaries almost always employ their visions merely to express their hopes and fears, rather than using the future as a narrative space for the disinterested exploration of possibilities; he names H. G. Wells as the sole exception to that rule. Although Derennes is careful to anchor his own scientific romance firmly in the contemporary world—as Wells routinely did—leaving its futuristic implications within the realms of potentiality, he does seem to have been attempting to answer France's complaint, by exploring a possibility that he neither desired nor feared, in a detached and purely hypothetical mannĐespite its clear Wellsian influence, *Le peuple du Pôle* remains solidly Vernian in its formulation as a romance of exploration. If one of its two principal literary models is Wells' *The First Men in the Moon* (1901), the other is Verne's *Voyage au centre de la Terre* (1864; tr. as *Journey to the Center of the Earth*). As in Wells' novel, Derennes tells the story of two strategically ill-matched explorers who stumble upon an alien society whose organization and mores are sharply contrasted with those of human society, providing a challenging standard for evaluative comparison; as in Verne's,

6

the alien society is located in a subterranean enclave that has been isolated from the otherwise-worldwide scheme of biological evolution for millions of years. The most original component of Derennes' plot, and the element that is of most interest within the history of imaginative literature, is that he, unlike Verne—or Arthur Conan Doyle, who was to publish *The Lost World* five years later—makes the key assumption that progressive biological evolution would have continued in that enclave, to the extent that the iguanodons isolated there in the remote past have developed a quasi-humanoid form, along with high intelligence and sophisticated technological capability. The standard of comparison they provide, by virtue of the deft extrapolation of that hypothesis, is markedly different from that provided by Wells' Selenites, which are social insects writ large.

Derennes never wrote another scientific romance, although he did write other fanciful travelers' tales, including "*Les conquérants d'idoles*" (1908), here translated as "The Conquerors of Idols," which was reprinted as the title story of the collection *Les conquérants d'idoles et autres aventures* in 1920. He eventually published some 50 volumes of various sorts before dying in 1830—somewhat prematurely, as his father had before him—but he was never tempted back to Wellsian fiction. He did publish other fantasies, but they were mostly anecdotal tales in the same vein as "*Les conquérants d'idoles*," often based on motifs borrowed from Basque or Provençal folklore. His output was very diverse—it includes travel guides, "true crime" stories and a notable work on betting systems, *Le fortune et la jeu* [Luck and Gambling] (1926)—but his contemporary reputation was primarily based on two strands of concern. One is his regional fiction depicting the folkways of south-western France, which mostly deals with Basque culture, although he also published one volume of poetry in Occitan, the ancient language of southern France, which enjoyed something of a revival in the period. The other, which included his most successful works, consists of stories describing the lives of animals in an intimate but conscien-

7

tiously non-anthropomorphic fashion. These included a loosely-knit trilogy collectively entitled *Le bestiaire sentimental* [The Sentimental Bestiary] (1920-24), which won the Femina Award. The only book by Derennes previously translated into English is the middle volume of the trilogy, *La chauve-souris* (1922; tr. as *The Life of the Bat*). *Le peuple du Pôle* laid some significant groundwork for the latter work by casting human vanity and the human treatment of other species in a starkly objective and harshly unflattering light—a rhetorical purpose for which he also used some of his folkloristic fantasies, including *La petite faunesse* (1918).

The contemporary reader will observe, in reading this translation of *Le peuple du Pôle*, that the original was very much a product of its time, and that it reflects a particular moment in the history of aeronautics and the history of exploration, which was of brief duration. Modern history, with the invaluable aid of hindsight, now considers that the history of aviation was revolutionized in December 1903, when Orville and Wilbur Wright appear to have undertaken the first successful flight in a winged airplane, but that did not seem to be the case at the time, especially in Europe. The Wrights' first successful trial, if it did actually happen—there were few witnesses—was not repeated for some years, and their claim was initially treated with considerable skepticism. The most famous aviation pioneer based in Europe, the Brazilian aeronaut Alberto Santos-Dumont, did not redirect his attention from dirigible balloons to winged aircraft until 1907; his famous monoplane did not make its first flight until 1909. Derennes' novel is very specifically set in 1905-1906, when dirigible balloons were all the rage—especially, if somewhat hypothetically, in the context of polar exploration, which was likewise a topic of immense public interest.

Although Jules Verne and H. G. Wells provided the literary inspiration for *Le peuple du Pôle*, the historical inspiration was undoubtedly provided by the American journalist Walter Wellman (1858-1934). Wellman was not the first man to attempt to reach the North Pole in a balloon; as Derennes is careful to acknowledge and exploit in his story, the Swedish explorer Salomon-Auguste Andrée (born 1854) had set off in an attempt to reach the Pole in a balloon in 1897, and never returned. Wellman made his own first attempt to reach the Pole overland in 1899, but he eventually conceived much greater ambitions when he became ensconced as the Washington correspondent for the *Chicago Tribune*. He took advantage of the fierce circulation wars raging at the time—which gave rise to a large number of extravagant publicity stunts—to persuade his proprietor to put up a quarter of a million dollars to fund an attempt to reach the Pole by means of a new model dirigible. The initial organization of the expedition was loudly advertised in December 1905 and it subsequent progress—or lack of it—was profusely reported for the following three and a half years.

The much-publicized new design of Wellman's "advanced" dirigible, including its triple-ply envelope and double engine, is obviously the model for the one Derennes attributes to his own inventor, Ceintras, although Derennes is careful to add some further innovations. The plot of *Le peuple du Pôle* hinges on the fact that Ceintras and de Venasque are specifically attempting to steal Wellman's thunder; Derennes could not know, of course, that Wellman's dirigible would never actually succeed in traveling more than a few miles from its base camp in Spitzbergen, and that the project would eventually be abandoned in 1909, after Robert Peary claimed to have beaten Wellman to the target in April of that year, traveling overland. Peary's claim was probably false—it generated widespread skepticism and intense controversy at the time—but, whether it was true or not, it robbed Wellman's project of much of the publicity value derivable from its success, and the *Tribune*'s readers must have grown weary of the expedition's chronicle of continual delay and failure.

Although this topical relevance must have added considerably to the appeal of *Le peuple du Pôle* to its contemporary readers, it also ensured that the book became dated very quickly. By 1909, it was widely believed that the North Pole had been reached, and it had become obvious that the future of aviation belonged to winged aircraft rather than dirigible airships. This is presumably the principal reason why the novel was not reprinted in Derennes' lifetime, and has only been reprinted once since then, in a 250-copy edition produced by Jean-Pierre Moumon's small press Apex in 2002 (although a Spanish translation appeared in 1995). The original edition has become very rare; no copies were available for purchase on the Internet in 2007.

This relative neglect is unfortunate; dated as it may be, the novel remains a highly impressive example of French Wellsian fiction, and still retains much of its bite as a Voltairean *conte philosophique*. Its employment of a dirigible balloon is more likely to endear it to modern science fiction readers than to alienate them, given the contemporary fashionability of steampunk fiction, and the only aspect of the narrative likely to seem a trifle awkward to modern readers is the apologetic strategy that insists on stressing the unreliability of its narrators to a degree that some readers might deem excessive. Even that awkwardness has its charm, and the element of comedy added into the early part of the narrative to emphasize that the exercise is, after all, a mere *jeu d'esprit*, provides a firm fountain for the artful *bouleversement* that eventually transforms the internal narrative into a scathing exercise in satirical melodrama. As well as qualifying as a landmark work in the history of European scientific romance, therefore, the novel remains eminently enjoyable and intellectually challenging.

The translation of *The People of the Pole* has been made from the 2002 Apex edition, but that is reproduced photographically from the original edition and does not differ from it textually. I have made a couple of minor corrections to the text; it is conceivable that Derennes' misrendering of Walter Wellman's surname as "Wellmann" was deliberate, but I have assumed that it was an error and have altered it. Derennes also made a mistake—this one certainly not deliberate—in coupling Santos-Dumont's name with "les Juchmès." There was, in fact, only one Juchmes (whose name does not appear to have been ornamented by a *grave* accent), but he was the employee of two brothers, Paul and Pierre Lebaudy, who were the designers and constructors of the dirigible airship he piloted, so I have altered the reference to "the Lebaudys." I have made no other changes, save for the usual modifications of punctuation and syntax intended to make the text read more smoothly in English.

The translation of "*The Conquerors of Idols*" has been made from the version in the 1920 collection; I have not been able to compare this with the original periodical version. I have not made any corrections or other significant changes to the text, on the assumption that certainly manifestly incorrect details of the enclosed tale are deliberately attributed to the unreliable narrator by the author, who must have been aware that the Incas did not wear feather head-dresses of the kind routinely attributed to North American Indians and did not hunt or maintain domestic herds of "buffalo."

Brian Stableford

The People of the Pole

Prologue

This is merely a sort of preface, and in the chapters that follow, it is not me who will recount the story. As the revelations contained in this book will, however, run into an old prejudice of human vanity, it would be presumptuous on my part not to fear that the first impulse on the part of the public will be to see *The People of the Pole* as nothing more than a work of the poetic imagination or a novelist's game. I therefore wish to record my sources in advance, to explain where the story I have to tell came from. Moreover, I do not ask anyone to accept it meekly at face value; I shall be satisfied if its readers share the successive sentiments that I felt myself—which were: incredulity; then amazement; then the persuasion that what I had just read was possible; and then the certainty that there was no reason to doubt it.

There is an axiom that ought to be stated before going any further, since it indicates the departure-point of the dialectic to which one ought, in my view, to conform: it is that we pronounce the words "extraordinary" and "inadmissible" rather scornfully with respect to realities that the progress of intelligence and its means of investigation will perhaps permit us to observe experimentally tomorrow. It is certain that all savants—and perhaps all men, in the shadow of their fatal insufficiency—occasionally run into one of these innumerable verities, which seem to be consciously trying to evade them. To master of one of them often requires no more than a trifling adjustment. Humankind advances, but it advances at hazard, and the most unexpected horizons unveil themselves abruptly;

hypotheses that one scarcely dares support in the secrecy of dreams are suddenly transformed into objectively incontestable facts. It would probably only require a tiny increase in our means of telescopic or microscopic observation for science, religions and morals to be turned upside-down overnight.

In the month of September 1906, I happened to be in Saint Margaret's Bay, a village in the county of Kent, across the Channel from the Pas de Calais, some six miles from Dover. I had gone there with the intention of writing, in the peace of a region not yet profaned by excessively numerous hordes of tourists, an essay on "The Motor Car and the Modern Soul." My work was nearly finished; before returning to Paris, I was only waiting for the arrival of my illustrious friend Louis Valenton, a professor at the Collège de France and a member of the Institut. After returning from a long and difficult paleontological expedition in northern Asia, he was to spend a few days relaxing at Saint Margaret's Bay, and we planned to return from there to France together. On the evening of the 20th, I received a telegram informing me that he had just disembarked at Liverpool. The following day, I saw two trucks loaded with trunks pull up outside the lodgings where I was staying; a few minutes later, Louis Valenton descended in person from an ancient hired cab.

Louis Valenton is not only a savant of indisputable competence, but also a man of taste: an artist sensitive to the beauty of landscapes, who is able to describe and eulogize them in terms that many poets would envy. On the day after his arrival, therefore, he was not content to show me the paleontological specimens that he had discovered; he recounted the story of his journeys through the pine forests of Siberia, telling me about immense plains, hidden almost all the years round by a blanket of snow, desolate regions where scarcely anything grew but meager mosses, and where the eternal voice of the wind was the only living thing, ravines whose vast blue-tinted scree-slopes seemed to be suspended over those who ventured into them, threatening them with the continual menace of landslides. He told me about sudden avalanches whose thunderous echoes in the vast solitudes reverberated to infinity, and caverns whose depths enclosed a darkness hundreds of thousands of years old—and in which, before disinterring the scientific treasures of vestigial fossils, he had sometimes been obliged to remove heaps of carcasses devoured in the past by bears or wolves.

The expedition had been rewarding. In addition to well-preserved skeletons of extinct animals, of which only insignificant fragmentary remains had previously been recovered, he had brought back the bones of one creature that had never before been glimpsed or anticipated, and whose discovery would have unappreciable consequences for historians of the evolution of species. He opened a crate and took out some carefully-packaged and numbered bones, gleaming beneath the layer of whale-blubber with which he had smeared them after extracting them from the ground, in order to avoid their rapid pulverization.

Then, crouching on the floor, he rapidly reconstituted the skeleton, as children do with games of patience that have, in the fullness of time, become familiar to them. When the work was done, I could scarcely retain a cry of amazement, so curiously humanoid did the creature seem. Remembering my college days and certain articles I had skimmed through in journals, I exclaimed: "An anthropopithecus!"

Valenton smiled, and shook his head negatively. "No," he said, "it's not the hypothetical creature with whose aid, for want of anything better, our savants have tried to bridge the abyss that still gapes between the anthropomorphic apes and primitive humankind! The hind limbs and the vertebral column are certainly disposed in such a manner as to leave no doubt of the possibility of a near-perfect vertical stance, and the cranial cavity is undoubtedly more highly-developed than that of gorillas, and even that of certain primitive peoples— but look at the skeleton a little more closely. Consider the unusual length of that neck; those sharp and conical teeth; the articulation of that shoulder, which only permits the arm to move in a vertical sense; those fore-limbs, which fold in an opposite direction to the human arm, like the feet of a swimming dog; those hands—for want of a better word—equipped with six fingers, scarcely able to grip, and probably linked together by membranes; that enormous tail in the form of a flipper; and, finally, the pelvic bones, so narrow and not at all humanoid. You'll see that this is no longer the famous ancestor of humans but an amphibious reptile, a denizen of the Tertiary marshes or seas, probably oviparous..."

Valenton went to the crate and withdrew some calcareous fragments, which he held out to me: "Here," he added. "Look at the imprints left on these rocks, on which the animal's bones were resting. It had no hair, and its skin must have borne a strange resemblance to that of lizards, as it appears to us under a magnifying-glass."

He fell silent momentarily, then went on: "At first, I too committed an error analogous to yours; I called the animal a pithecosaurus. You know that the mammals, like the birds, are the descendants of great primitive saurians, such as iguanodons, megalosaurs and plesiosaurs? Well, after a cursory examination, it seemed to me that the pithecosaurus must be to the first ape what the pterodactyl is to the archaeopteryx. Now, though, I've given the creature another name..."

In an emotional voice, almost holding my breath in anguished anticipation of an enormous revelation, I asked: "What?"

"The anthroposaurus," Valenton replied. "Yes—you understand what the term *anthropos* signifies in that composite name. It isn't there to indicate a physical similarity, which, as I just pointed out to you, is quite superficial; it's there, for want of anything better—intelligence and reason being, on Earth, the exclusive attributes of the human race—to indicate that the creature was indubitably endowed, to some degree, with reason and intelligence."

He stressed the word *indubitably*, and repeated it as he took the skull in his hands, considering it intently. "Cuvier," he said, "reconstituted certain extinct animals in their entirety

16

after examining a limb or a jawbone, and the discovery thereafter of complete skeletons almost always demonstrated the exactitude of his reconstructions. Well, I tell you, on my own authority, that it is sufficient to look at this skull and measure that facial angle to deduce with near certainty that a degree of reason and intelligence, the primary elements of a religion, a morality and an organized social existence are consequential thereupon."

"Then intelligence must have preceded human beings on Earth?" I exclaimed.

"No," Valenton replied. "This animal is contemporary with the first humans. Human intelligence and anthroposaurian intelligence must, at one time, have existed concurrently. Here—this is a comparison that seems to me to give a rather good account of the fashion in which species evolve, are transformed and give rise to one another. Imagine a family that owns a house in a fertile region. The fields that it owns provide its nourishment, feeding the first children, and perhaps the children of those children, but, as the family grows, the domain is no longer sufficient; soon, the new generations are forced to see their fortune elsewhere. These people then become what the nature of their adoptive homeland requires them to be; if, for example, the land is covered with forests that are difficult to clear, and in which animals are abundant, they become hunters instead of agriculturalists like their brothers and cousins who remain in the cradle of the family.

"In the same way, leaving the primitive marshes where the monstrous saurians of previous ages lived, certain species gradually colonized firm ground and became covered with hair; they are the ones from whom the various kinds of mammals descended. But the fraternal species that remained in the marshes continued nevertheless to transform themselves in a progressive manner. Is there anything astonishing in the possibility that, in the meantime, one or more of them came into possession, like the human species, of a brain endowed with reason and intelligence—the culminating point of the progress that we can presently imagine for a living being?"

I recall continuing this conversation with Valenton, a short while afterwards, in the lodging-house's little arbor, accompanied by tea steaming in white and blue china cups. Flocks of seagulls were skimming the surface of the sea, scarcely rippled by an imperceptible breeze. On the chalk-white cliffs, crowned by green meadows, pretty cottages were aligned along the coast to the right and the left; in the distance, a little steamer—a black dot plumed with smoke—was disappearing in the direction of France. That evening was the most peaceful and mildest of Earthly evenings—but how far I was from that familiar reality! My mind had retreated through the Ages; I imagined the strange creatures whose discovery Valenton had revealed to me, in a setting of gigantic tree-ferns, on the edge of a marsh swarming with tumultuous life, under an ancient terrestrial sky still fully impregnated with heat and humidity. I seemed to see the first humans—huge, hairy and cruel, armed with sharp-edged stones—advancing carefully upon the anthroposaurians, with the vague intention of annihilating that rival race.

"We can no longer assert, now," I said, "that, if man is the king of Earthly creation, his is a royalty of divine right; he has obtained that kingship by right of conquest. There being various intelligent species, or species bearing within them the possibility of the intelligence that would one day exist on our planet, it was necessary that one should triumph—and that was ours..."

My mind spurred itself on, galloping like a colt running freely over a prodigious new field that has suddenly opened up before it; a crowd of ideas and images appeared pell-mell, in confused abundance, as that course proceeded at hazard. Myths were clarified; legendary creatures were explained. I understood then what undines and sirens had been; I no longer saw, in the story of Cain and Abel, anything more than a symbol of the struggle in consequence of which Human-Cain had sacrificed Anthroposaurus-Abel to his desire for absolute dominion. And I talked and talked, my voice becoming more excited and feverish with every passing minute.

Then Valenton, with a smile, put his hand on my shoulder and informed me, in a slightly mocking tone, that I was going a bit too far.

"Now, my dear friend, you're straying into the realm of pure fantasy. It seems to me, though, that it's easy to draw conclusions that are more interesting, scientifically speaking, from the existence of the anthroposaurus. One is entitled to say, for example, that instead of one king of creation on the Earth, there might have been two or more of them, if the species had lived so far apart as not give offence to one another. Thus, Christopher Columbus, on discovering America, instead of finding a new human race there, might have encountered beings entirely different from humans, but just as intelligent and rational, with their own cities, their own laws, similarly believing in God—or having decided, sooner than humankind, no longer to believe in Him..."

"Yes," I said, "but nowadays, there is no longer any tiny fraction of our narrow Earth that is unknown to us. We can therefore be certain that the victory of humankind has been brutal and definitive; if intelligent creatures physically different from us exist, we must resign ourselves to imagine them on another world in space—on the planet Mars, for example." And I added, laughing rather coarsely: "Ah, yes, the planet Mars! Here's a good opportunity to talk about those famous Martians again!"

Valenton looked me full in the face and said, quite seriously: "Think about what you're saying. Are you quite sure that the entire Earth is known to us? Including the depths of the sea? Including—above all—the immense regions that extend beyond the polar ice-sheets? Besides, you're sufficiently familiar with the scientific method to know that it's even more futile, in confrontation with the unknown, to deny than to affirm, since, where facts that are not yet experimentally observable are concerned, we can deduce, if not certainties, at least possibilities founded on inductive reasoning..."

"The anthroposaurians, or their descendants," I suddenly exclaimed, "still exist somewhere!"

How had I arrived at that idea before Valenton had given me any indication of the end to which his mild rebuke was directed? Had I divined the conclusion from the tone of his voice, serious and triumphant at the same time? Was it that, having seen the skeleton of that singular monster of past ages, and having learned what it was, I was fully prepared to accept, and even to expect, other revelations even more extraordinary or unprecedented? I don't know. In any case, I hasten to say that my interruption had been rather thoughtless and my conjecture somewhat exact.

"What a child you are, decidedly!" said Valenton. "You go from one extreme to the other with disconcerting ease. No, there are probably no more anthroposaurians, either in the depths of the sea, at the pole or anywhere else...but *somewhere*, there is *something*..."

From one of his pockets—which were always bulging with pamphlets, books and pieces of paper—he took a thick bundle, which he held out to me.

"Read that," he added. "I brought something back from my voyage other than bones dating back millions of years. These papers were enclosed in a very modern object, in one of those petrol cans that our motorists can buy any day of the week at a garage door! I ought to tell you that if I had found that object in a ditch, in the suburbs of London or Paris, my paleontologist's mind would not have paid much attention to the banal modernity—but out there, in the muddy ice of the shore of the Yalmal peninsula, near the mouth of the Ob, the encounter could only be unexpected. Having established that the can wasn't empty, after a moment's hesitation, I attached it to my luggage. I believe that I have grounds for self-congratulation. On the boat that brought me back I took it apart and extracted these papers; they had been slipped into it one by one, carefully numbered, through the narrow opening. I sorted them out immediately and quickly read through them. No—don't ask me anything; read them yourself..."

He smiled briefly at my impatient curiosity, then added: "Read them yourself and publish them. You know that I'll have enough work to do this winter assembling my fossil bones and writing my report. As you see, you'll be doing me a service..."

As soon as I got back to France, I set to work. The sheets of paper were covered in a hurried script, written in pencil; it was horribly difficult to decipher in places. I think, though, that I have accomplished my task with all desirable attentiveness and conscientiousness, and am offering my readers a transcription that is as satisfactory as possible.

Furthermore, I notify those who, after closing this book, remain incredulous, that I retain the original manuscript at home, which is at their disposal, along with the petrol can brought from the Yalmal by Monsieur Louis Valenton, member of the Institut and Professor of the Collège de France. I hope that the reputation of my illustrious friend and the elevated position he occupies in the scientific world will prevent them from persisting any longer in the idea that they are faced with a vulgar hoax.

I. Two Men, Two Chimeras

My name is Jean-Louis de Venasque. I belong to an old Navarraise family descended from a companion of Henri IV, who fought by his side at Arques and Ivry and subsequently obtained, as a reward for his services, the title of Comte de Venasque and the lordship of Orio. Our name often crops up in chronicles, and even in the history of Old France. There is every reason to fear, alas, that it will disappear after me, not merely from history but even from the registers of the civil estate.

Since the Revolution, the last surviving branch of our family has lived, regretful of past splendors and glories, in our hereditary château at Orio. I was born on April 4, 1872. My father was then nearly 40. I see him, in the very first memories of my earliest childhood, dressed in summer and winter alike in a double-breasted coat of nankeen velvet, with a large felt hat and coarse leather gaiters, always carrying—except during meal-times or when he was asleep—a rifle and bandolier. I don't think he had ever known any other pleasure than that of the hunt and I don't recall having heard him string ten words together on any subject other than his cynegetic exploits.

All year long, he scoured his estates and the remote wilderness of the mountains, indiscriminately killing crows and partridges, foxes and hares, bears and smugglers. In his later years, he came to prefer smugglers to any other prey, and that was doubtless what caused his downfall; one night, he did not return to the château and was found a few days later lying by the side of a mountain stream, his face half-eaten by crows and his chest punctured by two bullets. The vengeance that had been so long in coming had eventually arrived. It is necessary to be careful of human prey.

My mother, a pious and timid person, was of modest origin; my father had, at the time, married for love. After this tragic event, the idea having undoubtedly occurred to her that her husband had died without confession, she had no other end in life but to save his soul by prayer, and confined herself to meticulous devotion. The squires of the neighborhood, and their wives especially, stopped coming to visit us when the Comte was no longer there to guarantee the dignity of the house, for my mother had always been considered an intruder in their society. She did not care, being absorbed by her pious practices, indifferent to anyone but herself. I only saw her at meal times, when she scarcely spoke a word to me. Two old servants took care of me, and I was free to seek my pleasure wherever I might find it, on condition that I did not leave the grounds; all the doors were kept locked. It was feared—and with reason—that the smugglers from the mountains might seek further vengeance against the son of their former executioner.

To understand my destiny, it is necessary to understand the child I had been. It is necessary to see me eternally enclosed by the double prison of the locked grounds and a narrow horizon of mountains. I do not think that anyone in the world knew the meaning of the word *ennui* better than I did, or was subject as completely as I was to certain consequences of that state of mind. Condemned to see the same objects perpetually, I invented marvelous countries and creatures beyond the inexorable wall of the mountains, among which my mind wandered. There was only one possible conclusion to all those dreams: "When I am grown up, I shall go away; I shall go to see what there is in the countries beyond the mountains."

Thus I developed, by degrees, an insatiable need for adventure—and when I finally left my prison, the conditions of my life having been modified, that desire was conclusively implanted within me. My habit of planning voyages lived on, as a cause that took hold of me. More than that: although my prison no longer existed, I contrived to see it everywhere, with an unconscious desire thus to maintain my desire for escape in all its ardor. That was easy for me to do between the four walls of the school to which my tutor sent me when my mother died; before I even entered adult life, I was perfectly certain that I would consider myself an eternal prisoner—a prisoner of the towns and countries to which my desires and tastes, friendship and love might attach me. Besides, having read books and pursued out my studies, I no longer even had consolation of imagining that there were new and extraordinary things in distant countries. Men had visited them all, explored them all, violated the wildernesses and recounted their travels. And the Earth entire—the Earth from which no manner of escape was possible—appeared to me as an immense prison, presently and forever.

What good would it do to go away, what good would it do to visit the countries about which I had once dreamed, since I was condemned eternally to follow in the footsteps of others? I had arrived too late on our planet; mystery had been banished everywhere. When I thought about the destiny of a Christopher Columbus or a Vasco da Gama, I experienced in the secrecy of my heart the most atrocious and most desperate sentiment of envy—and that strange mental malady was further exaggerated with every day that passed.

My dream, which I then believed to be unrealizable, had taken a precise and much more cruel form in my mind; it had, so to speak, crystallized out in a few words that I repeated to myself incessantly: "To see what human eyes have never seen!" That became the obsession and torture of my every waking moment.

In my house, in the streets, in the countryside, I was perpetually afflicted by the atrocious illusion that the gazes imposed on objects by generations of human beings remained attached to them, like stains, which I could detect, almost visibly. Nothing seemed to me to be fresh, new, or worthy of consideration without disgust—not even the heart of a flower opening at daybreak, not even the tip of the shoot breaking through the soil, not even an infant's smile...

The days went by. I had neither relatives nor friends, and I lived wrapped up in myself, face to face with my obsession. Fearful of being taken for a madman if I revealed the cause of my sadness to anyone, I never let slip any confidence; for ten years, I was alone in supporting the weight of my thoughts.

Finally, one day, in the café to which idleness and ennui drew me on a daily basis, I happened to run into Jacques Ceintras. He had been my fellow, almost my friend, at college, but we had lost contact with one another a long time before. We chatted. After evoking banal communal memories for an hour or so, we abandoned ourselves to more intimate confidences regarding our present circumstances. Ceintras told me his life story. After leaving the Ecole Centrale, he had been obliged, for lack of a personal fortune, to accept a job as an engineer in a steelworks in the Vosges; his situation was good, his future assured, but he was not happy; all the time, he dreamed of doing something else…

I looked at him, and, when he repeated in a melancholy fashion, "All the time I dream of doing something else…" I felt myself drawn towards him by an abrupt sympathy. He too was a dreamer, vainly pursuing the realization of his dream!

"Yes," he continued, "there's a question that has always preoccupied me: that of the conquest of the air. When I was at school, I scribbled plans for aircraft and dirigible balloons in my exercise books. My one hope then was to devote my life to carrying my research to a successful conclusion. As you see, though, I've temporarily accepted an existence that monopolizes my time, not leaving me a minute of liberty; the days go by, and nothing new happens. Already, full of anguish, I can sense the hour of resignation approaching: the definitive renunciation of projects too noble and too beautiful!"

He collected himself momentarily, and then went on more calmly: "Besides, I'm probably wrong to complain. There are, so to speak, appointed times for inventions that mark a new triumph of human beings over the laws of Nature, or their own nature; numerous inventors, without being aware of one another, in various parts of a country or the world, work simultaneously towards the same end, in silence, as if a mysterious password had been given. Among the number of seekers, there is always as least one favored to attain the goal towards which they are all working. The results that Santos-Dumont and the Lebaudys have obtained must console me for not having studied and resolved the question personally. But they say that one is never satisfied! Dirigible balloons exist now, which men are able to navigate through the air at will, attached to frail bubbles of gas. I have a potential application of that discovery in mind, and—until it presents itself to someone else, who will realize it instead of me—it will be a new regret, a new torment in my life…"

"What is it?" I asked.

"To reach one of the Poles in a dirigible balloon," he replied. "Yes, it's an enterprise than was justly considered reckless and chimerical in Andrée's time, when airships were slaves to the wind, but I'm convinced that it could now be undertaken in a dirigible balloon, carefully constructed with the benefit of scientific knowledge, with every chance of success."

It is as well to note that my meeting with Ceintras took place in February 1905 and that no mention had yet been made, at that time, of the Wellman expedition. This was, therefore, a true revelation for me; the prospect of a marvelous possibility was abruptly unveiled before me, and the hope that had fled so many years before brought back my smile.

"I'm rich, my friend," I exclaimed, shaking Ceintras' hand warmly. "If you wish, I shall advance the necessary funds for the experiments and the construction of the apparatus, and we shall set off together for the Pole!"

For a minute or so, he evidently thought that he was dreaming, or that I was mad, or that he was mad—but I was already telling him my life story, revealing to him the malaise from which I was suffering, and I soon sensed the confidence born within his mind and saw his eyes sparkling with joy.

"How much do you expect the expenses of the expedition to come to?" I asked.

He named an enormous figure, more than half my fortune—but what did that matter to me? Imagine a sick man who thinks himself doomed, to whom a physician offers the chance of a cure. Carried away by the excitement that follows unexpected strokes of luck, I don't believe I gave a moment's thought to the practical difficulties of the enterprise. I was as sure of the result as if the balloon had been constructed and was ready to depart...and I was sure, too, that after having satisfied my prideful desire, after having contemplated the last virgin country on Earth, I would no longer yearn for anything, that I would be cured, able to live without being the slave of a new insensate dream, able to live like ordinary men—finally, to live!

Blessing the chance that had saved two men by bringing them together, Ceintras and I suddenly embraced one another, without any thought of where we were, or how grotesque it might seem to the spectators, who must have noticed our expansive gestures and loud voices, and who doubtless thought that we were drunk. We were, indeed drunk on joy and hope, and we were staggering slightly as we left the café, to the accompaniment of laughter, arm-in-arm.

We did not leave one another all that night; we walked for kilometers along sleeping streets without feeling tired, our hearts and mouths full of plans. On the following day, we would get to work! And we went on talking, continuing our hallucinatory march at hazard. At the first light of dawn, we found ourselves on the summit of Montmartre; we emerged from the night as if from the most beautiful of dreams—a dream whose reality would be prolonged...

Leaning on the balustrade in front of the Sacré-Coeur, we looked out over the bell-towers, domes and roofs gradually emerging from the darkness. The last gas-lamps were going out, but their hesitant light had already been replaced by the dazzling reflections of the Sun's rays, lighting up windows here and there. Finally, the city appeared in its entirety, while the last shadows vanished in roseate and gilded mists; it seemed marvelously beautiful, as new to my eyes as if some magician had rebuilt it from top to bottom during the night. And thus it was, for the first time in years, that I saw the day break with a radiant heart.

II. The Cavaliers...

For some days, I considered Ceintras as my savior, and Ceintras returned the compliment—but it must be admitted, alas, that the honeymoon of enthusiasm and gratitude did not last.

I have neither the desire nor the leisure to put my unfortunate collaborator on trial here. I cannot, however, forget all the wrangling and arguments of which he was the cause and which were the bane of my life during the period of experiments. The disappointments he had experienced for some years had embittered his character and exalted his pride, which perennially took on the appearance of the most ridiculous sensitivity. Patience has never been my dominant virtue and, at the present moment, one of the things that astonishes me most is that I did not give it all up, including the hope of a cure, rather than endure, as I had to do for days on end, the enforced company of such a hateful individual. While destiny dragged us to our doom, however, we got past all the obstacles that our nature seemed to interpose between our plans and their realization with surprising ease, almost without noticing them.

At the outset of my relationship with Ceintras, when giving him the funds, I had exacted a promise of absolute discretion from him. I was determined that all the preparations should be accomplished in silence. This resolution was the consequence of my maniacal reasoning, crazy and meticulous at the same time. It seemed to me that if other people caught wind of our attempt, the desire would immediately strike them to get in ahead of us. It seemed to me that those suffering from the same malady as I was must be very numerous, on a worldwide basis; as the remedy did not exist in sufficient quantity, the polar regions being the only unexplored territories remaining on Earth, I was quite determined to reserve it entirely for myself.

Naturally, Ceintras accepted this condition to begin with; he would meekly have accepted any conditions that reason or fantasy might have caused me to dictate to him. Gratitude swelled his heart to the same extent that banknotes swelled his pockets. It did not take him long, however, to repent of his promise and to make every effort to get out of it. Whatever he had said on the day that we met, his passion for scientific discovery was not solely inspired by concern for the interests of humankind; there was a healthy measure of the desire for glory in it. Ceintras dreamed of reporters laying siege to his door, of his name being displayed in large letters on the front pages of newspapers, of his photograph being reproduced in all the magazines. He ended up naively confessing this ambition to me, and when he understood that I was firmly determined not to give him the satisfaction, his desire transformed itself into an obsession that was probably as painful as mine had been.

He could no longer sleep or eat; he even seemed to lose interest in his work for a while. Sometimes, when I came into his workroom unexpectedly, I saw him hastily hiding pieces of paper; later, I recovered a few from his waste-basket; the unfortunate fellow, unable to read eulogistic articles written about him, was writing them himself, speaking in enthusiastic terms therein of Monsieur Ceintras, the young and brilliant engineer who was about to undertake the conquest of the Pole. I imagine that he learned them by heart and then recited them with his eyes closed, in the hope of maintaining the illusion!

I was, as I was entitled to be, annoyed by the delay that this discouragement and puerility brought to the execution of our plans. I sometimes said to Ceintras, as gently and amicably as possible: "The sooner we leave, the sooner we'll return, and the sooner you'll possess that glory you cherish so much! I have no intention of obliging you to keep the secret once we've come back!"

Usually, he replied, peevishly: "There you go! Not letting any opportunity pass to remind me that I'm under your orders and in your employ! Admit that you're in a hurry to finish and that you think I'm costing you too much. I like clear explanations, you know, old chap; if you're repenting your generosity, you have only to say so—I'd like that better!" And he would go off in a huff, shrugging his shoulders and slamming the door.

For my part, equally haunted by an obsession, I maintained a careful watch on his comings and goings. I dreaded that, if I lost sight of him for a single instant, he would take his notes to the newspapers and fill all the trumpets of fame with rumors of our impending exploit. I lived with him; I accompanied him everywhere, to the suppliers and the contractors. No jealous lover ever dogged his mistress's footsteps so obstinately! Naturally, this suspicion, of which he quickly took the measure, exasperated him, and he took his revenge as he could—by seeking, for instance, to addresses the most cruel and insulting words to my face.

"So you're afraid," he sometimes said to me, "that I might be skimming off a little cream? My dear friend, I pity your cooks!"

The balloon was finished, though. I can still see Ceintras displaying the sketches before my eyes, covering the blackboard with figures and formulae. "That'll do the trick," he said. To tell the truth, my knowledge of science being limited to the memories that remained from my school days and the meager profits that I had since extracted from a few desultory conversations with Ceintras, I was quite incapable of subjecting the assumptions on which he had based his apparatus to any serious critical examination on my own behalf. I had to wait for the experiments, and the wait was not without apprehension. Not that I ever doubted the worth of Ceintras—but the overexcited and resentful state of mind that he had been in from the outset of the enterprise had obviously not allowed him to exercise his faculties as a researcher and engineer in ideal circumstances.

My anxieties were justified. We had established our aerodrome in a little village in Beauce, two hours from Paris. In the minds of the local peasants, who were vulgar folk dulled by prosperity, insolent and sly at the same time, we were "the two crazy Parisians who were building a flying-machine." We were subjected by these brutes to a stupid and mocking hostility that was scarcely masked in their attitude by the respect that they were nevertheless obliged to render to people "who pay well."

The first ascent took place on April 15. It was immediately evident that, even if our apparatus was better than other dirigible balloons, we could not possibly depend on it for a journey that would last a week, at the very least. It was primarily a question of ballast, to which insufficient consideration had been given. We therefore limited ourselves—using three bell-towers as reference-points—to an aerial circuit of about 50 kilometers. This circuit was undertaken 18 times consecutively, at a mean velocity of 30 kilometers an hour; after that, or provision of ballast was exhausted. The balloon, whose weight was also increased by the humidity of the approaching night, slowly returned to Earth. We succeeded in maintaining a sufficient altitude for a little while longer, by throwing out a few cans of petrol and various objects representing the weight of indispensable accessories—observation apparatus, clothes and food—but that was obviously not a satisfactory solution, and we resigned ourselves to landing.

It would have been easy for me, after this failure, to take my revenge and remind Ceintras triumphantly of how annoying it would have been for him to inform the public too soon. His attitude did not permit it. He was not a bad fellow, deep down. He begged my pardon, shed all the tears in his body and spoke about dying. Yes, he did not want to survive his dishonor; he had not been worthy of my trust; I would have to find someone else. I reprimanded him sternly, gave him courage, and, in the end, something good came out of the check, because Ceintras renounced his arrogance, vanity and insolence for a while and went furiously back to work.

My troubles were not over, though. We had decided that the trial of the second balloon would have to take place somewhere near the Arctic regions, in order that the climatic conditions during the experiments and the journey would be very nearly the same. We chose Kabarova, a Samoyed village situated south of the Jugor Strait, at the entrance to the Kara Sea. It was the same village in which, 12 years earlier, Nansen had had his last contact with humankind before plunging into the heart of the polar wilderness.

By the beginning of July, the second balloon was complete. All our preparations had been made; ten workmen and an interpreter awaited our orders; the hydrogen apparatus, canisters of compressed gas and casks of provisions were heaped up in the baggage office at the Gare du Nord. It only remained for us to dismantle and pack up the balloon, when Ceintras coolly announced to me one morning that he was in love with a young woman and that his fixed intention was to marry her immediately!

I remember searching my pocket for a revolver, with the idea of threatening to blow Ceintras' brains out if he did not immediately promise me to postpone this reckless project until our return from the Pole, but I did not have a revolver. There were terrible scenes for two days; then, Ceintras having promised to leave a week after the wedding, I decided that the quickest way forward was to give in and expedite the business as soon as possible. Fortunately, the young woman's parents, and the young woman herself, did not want to hear any more talk of marriage once they knew that Ceintras intended to undertake a polar voyage a week later. The whole thing was conclusively broken off when he admitted to them—in strictest secrecy, in the hope of appearing as a hero in their eyes—the circumstances in which the expedition would be accomplished.

One might suppose that my poor friend, frustrated and distressed as he was, was not exactly an agreeable traveling companion, but I scarcely paid any attention to that. I thought that my troubles were finally at an end, and that Ceintras' ill-will, or vexatious character, had been rendered powerless. I told myself that, once we were installed at Kabarova, he would obvious be content to make careful preparations for the success of our enterprise—and it was, in fact, rather difficult to imagine whence, in the wilderness of the tundra, a wind might come that would fill his head with some new whim.

At first, events seemed to justify these optimistic expectations. The day after our arrival, we began to erect the hangar in which our airship would be sheltered and started the piece-by-piece assembly of the airship, despite the fatigue of a long journey that had eventually been completed with the aid of indescribable vehicles, the best of which were reserved for our provisions and our apparatus.

Our workmen, to whom we had communicated our intentions, assisted us with admirable devotion and enthusiasm; the reasoned struggle of Man against Nature has nowadays taken on all the appearance of a religion, and it was with a will analogous to that of cathedral-building masons that they set about establishing the machine that was to strip the Earth of one of its last secrets.

As for our hosts, they were stout fellows, marvelously pious, drunken and simple-minded. During the Sunday afternoons we spent at Kabarova, we saw them, under the direction of the three sordid monks who were maintaining the Orthodox faith in this remote region, carrying out interminable processions, during which their well-lubricated throats intoned ineffable hymns pleading for forgiveness, in honor of the icons that their unsafe hands transported beneath reindeer-skin canopies.

On other days, the population of the village spent long hours studying us, men women and children seated on the ground, confronting us unremittingly with broad smiles oiled by the slices of seal-blubber that they gobbled continually, with calm and insatiable appetites. The interpreter having told them that our intention was to fly up into the sky, higher than the birds, their sympathy was transformed into a respectful and fearful adoration, and they began then to murmur monotonous chants around us, which they accompanied by clapping their hands—and which we soon discovered to be chants in praise of our merits. All that did not prevent us from keeping an eye on them or posting a guard on our petrol cans—from which they would have drunk, for want of anything better, had the opportunity presented itself, settling up by subsequently doubling their devotion to our cause.

Once the hangar was established, a week's steady work sufficed for the completion of the balloon's assembly. While my enthusiasm increased in proportion to the progress of the preparations, however, Ceintras, for his part, let himself slide further and further into bleak depression. It was not that he did not make every effort to bring the enterprise to a successful conclusion, but he seemed to be accomplishing it with the conscientiousness and resignation of an imposed duty rather than acting under the impulse of the enterprising and intoxicated folly of an explorer or an inventor who sees himself near to arriving at his goal. He was far from the excited and fervent Ceintras of the evening when we had met! He spent long hours with the workmen, giving them orders, examining the least parts of the apparatus with a minute care that reassured me—for it made his evident desire to succeed manifest—but then, when he paused to rest, he declared himself tired out and went to sleep immediately, or pretended to sleep, thus avoiding all conversation with me.

Sometimes, in the grip of a slight anxiety with respect to his discouraged attitude, I pointed to the balloon and asked him: "Will it be all right?" He invariably replied, in a bland and expressionless voice: "It'll do the trick."

On the fifth day, though, he suddenly seemed to take it upon himself to slow the workmen down. He increased the rest-periods, saying that he had run out of energy; then, when I nagged him, begging him to get back to work and reminding him that the season was getting on, he went back to the workplace and dismantled some part of the apparatus on a vain pretext, which he then had to reassemble—to the extent that our balloon threatened to become reminiscent of Penelope's weaving.

On the seventh day, as I was asking myself anxiously what would happen next, Ceintras, incapable of containing the thoughts that were eating away at him any longer, raised his head from the task over which he was leaning, and brusquely said to me: "What if we put the expedition off until next year?"

I looked at him in amazement, but I understood immediately, by the fearful expression on his face, that he was defenseless in the face of an iron will. In a voice whose calm resolution even surprised me, I said: "That's impossible. Besides, it's too late now. The ship that has to come to find us is on its way." That very morning, in fact, determined to hurry events along, I had sent one of our men to the nearest telegraph station with a dispatch intended to alert the captain of the ship that was awaiting our orders in the fjord of Hammerfest in Norway, fully-equipped.

"You're right," he said. "It's better to finish it—and, if it's death that awaits us out there, not to prolong this atrocious agony."

The lamentable inconsistency of men! Ceintras, who, before he met me, had been crushed so many times by the black thought that he would never realize his dream of a polar expedition, was afraid of death now that destiny was on the point of fulfilling his avowed desire!

That evening, sitting on the threshold of our log cabin, he stared vaguely into the distance for a long time, as if hypnotized by the monotonous undulations of the wilderness that extended greyly in front of us, into infinity.

Unnerved by his immobility, I walked back and forth, whistling, with a mocking attitude that he would not have borne patiently in any other circumstances. He still seemed to be unaware of my presence. Finally, exasperated, I kicked his boot rudely and shouted into his ear, at the top of my voice: "Hey, Ceintras!"

I was immediately sorry that I had acted in such a cavalier manner; given Ceintras' irascible personality, anything might have happened. For the moment, though, he had better things to do than complain about my lack of courtesy. He looked at me as if he had woken up from a painful nightmare and, in a slightly uncertain voice, said: "So this polar expedition is going ahead? That's definite…"

Shrugging my shoulders, I simply relied: "Of course!"

He remained silent for a moment, and then, clenching his fists in a sort of impuissant rage, he shouted; "But for what? For what, for God's sake?"

"To see…"

"To see what?"

"Things that other men have not yet seen."

He released a sardonic laugh, desolate and scornful at the same time. Repeating the words that I had just said, he added an ironic exaggeration to their inspired tone.

"Things…things that other men have not yet seen! But what do you expect to find out there? Come on, tell me!"

"We'll know when we get there."

"When we get there! Well, do you want to know what I think, deep down? You're nothing but a madman. Pride has made you lose your head, the conceit of believing yourself too superior to the rest of humankind to be content with what suffices for them. In truth, yes, a madman and a conceited fool."

"A conceited fool! Oh, it seems to me that on that point, you…"

"And why's that? Just because, on the eve of undertaking an expedition as perilous as this one, I decide, at last, not to disappear into the unknown, in the middle of the ice-cap?"

I knew that there was no point in debating with Ceintras—that all the reasons I could give him, however good they might be, would only serve to irritate him further. Besides, I had no reasons to give him; we were merely executing the tacit contract that we had made when we first met, and his recriminations were arriving too late for me to take any account of them. So, without occupying myself any further with him, I set about leafing through the newspapers that reached us on a regular basis, but which we scarcely bothered to read, each of us being absorbed by a single thought….

Suddenly, my gaze was caught by these lines:

We are informed that the editor of an American newspaper, Mr. Wellman, has made a bold plan to reach the North Pole in a dirigible....

Followed by the commentary that everyone at that time was able to read in the press.

Then I held the journal out to my companion, underlining the passage with my fingernail, and cried out in a voice that made him tremble: "There, imbecile—read that! Just read..."

He accepted the newspaper indifferently, casting his eyes over it negligently—and his face was transformed, becoming animated as he read on. Ah, you should have seen my Ceintras, with the typical inconstancy of his mood, suddenly pass from the most utter discouragement to the most feverish excitement...

"Oh, no!" he exclaimed, after visibly hesitating between several ways of expressing himself. "That's good, that—it's very good! No, but how funny do you think it would be and how upset he'd be if this Wellman, at the very moment of his departure, learned that others had anticipated his scheme. For we'll be able to return before he leaves! And if he's absolutely determined to do something new, he'll have to set off for the South Pole! Ah, the South Pole! But who will have had the idea first? That's Ceintras—Ceintras!"

And he finished up singing these last words while dancing around and clapping his hands, to the amazement of the workmen, who doubtless suspected him of having indulged in excessively copious libations. Then, calmed down somewhat by these ridiculous demonstrations, he returned to the desire that had tormented him for so long, and said to me, affecting a detached tone: "We might perhaps send a telegram to the newspapers to notify them of our departure? We obviously have a good chance of success, but after all, what if we don't come back?"

"If we don't come back, as I've often repeated without your wanting to hear me, our workmen, after a two-month interval, will communicate the wills that we shall draw up before departure, and the crew of he ship that will carry us to the departure-point will also be there to attest to the truth."

He ended up allowing himself to be convinced that all this would be satisfactory, and ran to the work-shed, turning out crates, giving orders, frightening the workmen, working doggedly himself and cheerfully singing the opening couplet of *Viens, Poupoule!* [1]

I was obliged to drag him away by force to make him take a little nourishment. After the last mouthful, although our men were literally falling down with fatigue, he set to work again.

Two days later, the balloon was completely reassembled.

Disappointed or taciturn, Ceintras was merely annoying; having become joyful and expansive, he was unendurable. He threw himself upon me effusively, calling me his dear friend, heaping the manifestations of a sudden affection upon me, all of them punctuated by the intolerable *Viens, Poupoule!* whose every measure he underlined with clicks of his fingers or a few grotesque dance-steps. Oh, that odious refrain, his obsession with which survived so many adventures, and which still drones in my ears as I write these lines!

On the following day, we were to begin the period of ex-perimentation. In the meantime, Ceintras prepared the docu-ments destined to illustrate his glory. I had to photograph him in the gondola, at the helm, surrounded by our workmen, on the threshold of the hangar, in all sorts of poses, in all sorts of costumes...and to every frame, he carefully stuck pieces of paper on which were inscribed the captions that he hoped to see, some day, reproduced in the magazines...

"Besides," he said to me, with imperturbable seriousness, "if, by chance, we get stuck somewhere, out there"—and his

---

[1] *Viens, Poupoule* was the signature tune of the popular singer Félix Mayol (1872-1941), who established himself in Paris in 1895 and remained an archetypal exponent of French *chanson* until his death; he rewrote the words at least five times, and it is still available, not merely on CD but as a ringtone.

hand gestured in a northerly direction—"these explanatory notes will be absolutely necessary."

Towards the end of the day, no longer hearing my comrade's song resonating in the vicinity, I was about to go in search of him when I saw him appear, escorted by the three monks from Kabarova and a horde of glistening and greasy Samoyeds. On perceiving me, Ceintras clicked his fingers and, as his only reply to the questions that I put to him, contented himself at first with singing his familiar refrain. Then, pointing to the three obsequious monks, who were smiling and quite incapable of understanding what he said, he cried in a comically-emphatic fashion: "Here! These respectable monks, informed by our interpreter that our departure was imminent, have assured him that they will gladly consent to bless our aerial vessel with a bottle or two of brandy. Their benediction is well worth that! Given the nobility of these people, I think they're equally deserving to partake of our generosity."

We dug out two liters of rum for the monks and a can of methylated spirit, which the Samoyeds immediately began to pass from hand to hand and mouth to mouth, emitting grunts of satisfaction.

"Quickly, quickly take a picture!" Ceintras shouted to me, perched on an armature beam.

The monks were keeling down beside him; the crowd, having entirely emptied the can, intoned its hymn pleading for forgiveness...

When it was all over, Ceintras, who expected posterity to take this burlesque solemnity seriously, gravely attached this note to the frame:

The inhabitants of Kanarova acclaim the bold aeronaut Ceintras, while he has his dirigible balloon blessed by the local clergy, with great ceremony.

III. ...And Their Mount

I wish that my mechanical knowledge were more extensive and more precise, so that I could give a genuinely useful description of our balloon at this point. My final wish is that the foolish enterprise of which we have been the victims might at least bear fruit for other people than ourselves.

To consider only the external appearance of the apparatus, it differed very little from the other dirigible balloons that have been constructed in recent years, except in its considerable size; it was 75 meters long and 20 meters wide at the broadest extent.

Its great originality consisted of a mechanism that allowed us to dispense completely with ballast and to prolong its sojourn in the atmosphere, in spite of that, for a very long time—much longer than any aircraft had done before us. The hot gases emitted by the motor were collected in a pipe that divided shortly afterwards into two branches. One of them carried the gas into the coiled tubes that encircled our cabin, performing the function of heating it. By means of the other— and this is where the innovation came in—the exhaust gases, before their conclusive expulsion into the open air, were diverted into a second system of coils located inside the envelope in a copper sphere; when the balloon became to descended to Earth, a tap whose opening could be varied allowed a sufficient quantity of gas to escape to heat the metal sphere to a temperature of 60 degrees Centigrade.

Thus, at our discretion, we caused the hydrogen to expand and augmented the ascensional force without any risk of ignition. In addition, six canisters of compressed hydrogen, similarly connected by tubes to the interior of the envelope, allowed us to avoid the annoyance of the progressive loss of gas during our journey. A turn of the tap as soon as the need became appreciable, and a new provision of hydrogen went to replace the gas that the six layers of strong silk and rubber had not succeeded in keeping completely imprisoned. All the ramifications of this complex tubing were furnished with valves commanded by levers; when the temperature in our cabin was sufficiently high and the balloon was floating at an adequate height, we let the gases escape into the open air with a deafening noise.

Having no need to encumber ourselves with useless ballast, we were able, without any risk, to make our aerial vessel exceedingly solid and comfortable. After various hesitations, Ceintras had resolved to mount the envelope in a light aluminum armature which obviously maintained a greater rigidity than could have been achieved with compensatory ballonets. As for the airship's stability, that was assured, as usual, by horizontal and vertical fins.

The cabin was a veritable little house divided into two parts; the forward part—which we called, rather pretentiously, the warming room—accommodated Ceintras, as pilot and mechanic. It contained taps for the reservoirs of oil, petrol and water, the manual controls, the compass and the steering-mechanism, which commanded a powerful rudder situated at the rear. One door opened to an uncovered walkway by which one could reach the engine itself. In the other part of the cabin were the crates of provisions, a narrow bed and the little electrical stove on which we prepared our meals. In these conditions the journey itself seemed sure to be nothing less than an agreeable and slightly banal pleasure-trip; we would certainly not endure any of the ordeals to which other explorers of the polar regions had had to resign themselves in advance: hunger, cold and anxiety regarding a long exile.

Our new motor, with an effective thrust of 100 horsepower, did not permit us to attain an average speed much superior to that of 25 kilometers an hour, for the second balloon was considerably larger and heavier than the first. To accomplish the feat of long-distance aerial navigation, Ceintras had, in the final analysis—and not without reason—preferred an engine with staying-power to one built for speed, a cruiser to a racer. All things considered, though, founding our calculations on the certainty of a minimum of 20 kilometers an hour, a week would be quite sufficient for us to accomplish the 2000-kilometer return journey. It was at the extremity of Franz-Josef Land that our Norwegian ship was to set us down and wait for us.

The time allowed for the ship's arrival at Kabarova left us without about a fortnight to spare. That gave Ceintras an excuse for one last tergiversation; it took place as we were climbing into the balloon's gondola to conduct the trials. "What if we've told the ship to come for nothing?" he suddenly said to me. "What if the balloon, for one reason or another, doesn't prove entirely satisfactory?"

"We're going regardless," I replied. "It's up to you to take all precautions to safeguard your glorious existence! Anyway, you told me yourself: it will do the trick. This isn't the moment to become a pessimist."

Anyway, as events were to prove forthwith, he had no motive to become one. The immense machine was resting on the ground, moored by cables and stakes. When the moorings were cast off, it did not leave the ground immediately; the ascensional force at the moment of departure did not surpass the dead weight of the apparatus. Once the motor was activated, however, the heated air in the copper sphere expanded the hydrogen in the envelope and the balloon began to rise. To control the rapidity of the ascent, as required, it was sufficient to inject an additional quantity of hydrogen, drawn from the reserve-canisters, into the envelope. As is evident, this mechanism not only permitted us to dispose of the ballast, it also gave us the precious ability to set down whenever it seemed appropriate and to set off again as we pleased.

There was such a pliant docility in the slow ascent of the machine, freed for the first time its chains and weights, that all sorts of powerful emotions—pride, admiration, an almost religious respect for ourselves and our achievement—made our hearts beat hectically. In truth, those triumphant minutes had not been bought too dear by the anxieties, the annoyances and the thousand exasperating difficulties that I had suffered for long months. When the decisive moment arrived, when we had attained sufficient altitude, and when Ceintras, momentarily sealing the tube by which warm air reached the envelope, had engaged the propeller, all our quarrels and disagreements were forgotten. Our hands clasped, while we searched in vain for appropriate words to express our happiness and mutual gratitude.

All that was a favorable augury, and suffice it to say that nothing gave the lie to it. I don't intend, at any rate, to describe our experiments in detail; that would be tedious and pointless. During the ten days that followed, the balloon covered more than 3000 kilometers and remained in working order, without it having been necessary to renew our provision of petrol or hydrogen. The slight misadventures that we had to endure only served to affirm and further increase our confidence. Once, 100 kilometers from Kabarova, our engine stalled because of an excess of oil and the clogging of the spark-plugs; the balloon landed softly, we carried out a rapid cleaning of the cylinders, and then the engine started up again; the balloon took off again and we returned to base camp after a delay of less than half an hour relative to our prearranged timetable. Only one important modification was made to the machine during these final days; we reinforced the shock-absorbers designed to avoid bumps during landings and arranged them in a different fashion, which would permit us to land without danger in extremely narrow spaces.

It would be equally pointless to describe our voyage from Kabarova to Franz-Josef Land. The slow navigation of the boreal seas; the opaque mists that seemed to have been there for centuries on end, which only opened reluctantly and sluggishly to let the vessel pass; the perpetual restlessness of the ice in the narrow channels of clear water as we drew nearer to the sheet; the icebergs floating in the distance like pallid shadows within the mist—all of that is familiar from the accounts of explorers, and has no purpose to serve within my story, especially when I think that my days are doubtless numbered.

The balloon, whose mechanical parts we had not needed to dismantle, was re-inflated and ready to depart five days after our disembarkation. It only remains for me to reproduce here the document written in duplicate, of which we kept one copy, the other being confided to the captain on the very eve of our departure.

On August 18, 1905 the Tjörn, *a Norwegian ship under the command of Captain Hammersen, deposited at the extreme southern tip of Franz-Josef Land, Messieurs Jacques Ceintras and Jean-Louis de Venasque, French subjects, both domiciled in Paris at 145A Avenue de la Grande-Armée, who departed from there on August 26 in an attempt to reach the North Pole in a dirigible balloon. Another document has been sent by them to Monsieur Henri Dupont, domiciled in Paris at 75 Rue Cujas, the chief of the crew of workmen who assisted them during the period of trials at Kabarova (Russia). In the case of success, Hammersen, captain of the* Tjörn, *H. Dupont and the other members of the crew will confirm the exactitude of the said documents. In the case of failure and the definitive disappearance of the two explorers, they are requested to divulge the facts to which they have been witnesses. Messieurs Ceintras and de Venasque request this divulgence, less for the satisfaction, although legitimate, of being inscribed in the number of victims of science as to offer an example and a lesson to those who, having subsequently conceived analogous plans in pursuance of the progress of aerial navigation, will be tempted to realize them in their turn.*

IV. Talk Between Heaven and Earth

"Cut the mooring-ropes!"

And after the abrupt sound of hatchet-blows, the cords fell one by one, clattering on the dry ground. The entire crew had accompanied us; hands were extended towards us; we were already in the gondola. Then there were a few minutes of impressive silence. The men had arranged themselves around us and were no longer moving.

I looked at them. Without a doubt, these sons of Vikings—those bold mariners who had crossed the Atlantic without knowing it, long before Christopher Columbus, in their red-painted open boats—sensed their hereditary desire for adventure stirring in the utmost depths of their being as they watched us depart. It was not only astonishment and admiration, but a naïve envy, an obscure regret at not being invited to the party, that brought a transitory sparkle to the pale eyes of those sailors of the Northern seas.

A dog that was still aboard the ship suddenly began to howl and I suddenly became aware that there was no turning back. I must have been very pale, but Ceintras was frightfully so; he advanced unsteadily towards the engine and I saw his fingers trembling beneath the thickness of his fur gloves as he pressed the lever to get us under way. Then, at that supreme moment, the image imposed itself on my mind of other countries, full of animation, sunlight, life…that was what we were leaving behind, perhaps forever! For a few seconds, I had a horrible certainty of having often come close to happiness without suspecting it, of having despaired of my cure too soon, and of being released as prey to darkness….

But the noise of the engine sheared through the silence, and we felt the cord and metal musculature of the immense beast trembling, impatient to be on its way. Eventually, it lifted suddenly from the ground, so quickly that Ceintras had to moderate the expansion of the hydrogen almost immediately. Then, drowning out the noise of the engine, a loud acclamation rose up from the ground, which reached us in flight; before that tempest of enthusiasm, my black notions and crushing thoughts dissipated, dispersed like dead leaves in the wind. Leaning over the walkway, I waved my hand one last time at the cheering crowd.

At that moment, the true grandeur of the work that I had accomplished unconsciously, with no other purpose than the satisfaction of an egotistical desire, became apparent to me: a marvelous windfall that I had not expected. As in the first moments of our trials, my heart beat hectically—and this time, the intoxicating impulsion was not merely due to the hope of the imminent realization of a dream, but to a better and sweeter sensation. From then on, whatever might follow, I was certain that I had not led a useless life, that I had been able, at the very least, to furnish the future and my fellow men with an illustrious example of initiative and audacious will.

Ceintras had also been visibly flattered and comforted by the acclamation, but his incorrigible vanity took his thoughts in a direction different from mine.

"What is this ovation," he suddenly cried, "compared with those that await us on our return?"

I could not help looking at him with a certain pity. Then the pity was succeeded by irritation. The ridiculous statement had broken the charm. For more than a quarter of an hour, the propellers had been active; the ship had already vanished behind us and the men, whose gazes were still following us, were no more than black smudges on the snow. To the limit of my vision, I could see nothing but the monotonous whiteness of the polar wilderness. The cold was beginning to seep into us and we went into the warming room, carefully closing the door behind us.

Then we discovered that we had nothing more to say to one another. Ceintras absorbed himself, silently, in the manipulation of the controls; for my part, after vainly attempting to start a conversation, I abandoned myself to the thread of a vague reverie. Soon, lulled by the monotonous noise of the engine and wearied by the fatigue of preceding days, I felt that I was gradually invaded by a profound somnolence. I think that I had arrived on the very edge of sleep when Ceintras suddenly tugged my sleeve and cried, peevishly: "I'm hungry!"

He muttered a few imprecations thereafter and I understood that he was complaining about the derelict manner which I was carrying out my duty. Was I not the expedition's chief cook?

Recognizing that the reproach was, in principle, justified—or too bewildered to muster any great desire to recriminate—I set to work to satisfy my companion's desire. I must admit that preparing our meal did not require any great culinary skill. Our provisions consisted primarily of economical nutriments—cocoa, tea, coffee, tablets of compressed meat—in biscuit form and various ready-to-eat conserves, which only required to be warmed up briefly in the bain-marie on our electric stove. Ceintras, who had no intention of being deprived even of superfluities, had added to all that various kinds of jam, dried cakes, liqueurs, vintage wines and champagne!

Shortly thereafter, I set out some biscuits on the bed—which was convertible and had also to serve as a table—along with two bottles of Bordeaux, a ham and some jugged hare; the odors ticked my nostrils in a most delightful manner.

"There you are!" I said, triumphantly. "A meal for which Nansen would have given a great deal, at certain points in his journey."

Ceintras, of course, did not share my opinion. The jugged hare was not warm enough; the Bordeaux should not be drunk so cold; the biscuits would certainly give him a stomach-ache...

With the best will in the world, though, I could not go in search of bread-rolls for him! In any case, grumbling all the while, he put at least half of the food away; I had no great difficulty in dealing with the rest. The copious repast was not sufficient for us, however, so we added some fruit jam and a healthy measure of rum. It should be noted at this point—a curious thing, given that we were not using up much energy—that we experienced a formidable appetite throughout the journey.

We enjoyed a very pleasant temperature in both parts of the cabin, and when our feast came to an end, we had a sensation of perfect well-being. From time to time, we used our sleeves to wipe away the thick mist and frost-flowers that accumulated on the portholes, but there was still the same monotonous landscape outside that explorers' narratives have rendered familiar. Under the influence of a feverish exaltation or a strange presentiment, however, I did not renounce my hope of seeing prodigies before much longer. Even though I anticipated ironic words and shrugs of the shoulders on Ceintras' part, I could not help expressing that hope immediately.

"Who knows, Ceintras, what we shall find at the end of our journey?"

"The axle of the Earth, of course," he eventually replied, sniggering.

"The axle of the Earth?" I repeated, in a questioning and rather skeptical tone.

"Oh, yes—you know very well that it starts out there, and we're rotating around it. We'll have to be careful not to break the handle by bumping into it, won't we? That would be cataclysmic!" Determined not to abandon such a good joke right away, he added: "I say—we could write our names on it, as tourists do in the keeps of historic castles. And we can still take away a few little pieces to give to our friends and acquaintances…."

Meanwhile, the enormous machine continued on its way with such perfect docility that I experienced an obscure sentiment of irritation. In truth, it was too easy, too simple. It seemed to me that a few slight obstacles would have contributed to increasing the value of our victory…

Exactly 33 hours after our departure, we passed the furthest point attained by Nansen and finally entered into the mysteries of virgin territory.

"Ceintras!" I cried, "Ceintras, this time we're really here!"

"Where are we, if you please?"

"In the heart of adventure, in the unknown....nothing, in the immemorial sequence of centuries, has disturbed the silence accumulated by this wilderness. This is the first time that this natural environment has ever been troubled by the prideful passage of man..."

"You're quite lyrical," Ceintras put in, without turning his head. "Deep down, you're still convinced that you'll have the opportunity, in a few hours, to contemplate marvels. Believe me, if you don't want to experience too great a disappointment, don't expect anything but what you see here. In a few hours, our instruments will indicate that we've reached our goal, and then..."

"And then, according to you, that will be all, and there'll be nothing left for us to do but go back?"

"You've said it. Meanwhile, by way of diversion—yes, if you like, so as not to have made the journey in vain, we can land briefly and plant the national flag on the very point of the Pole. The North Pole, French colony! Ah, what a pretty gift to offer one's fatherland! Once might insert a few announcements in the papers: *Estates to distribute, great opportunities for emigration...* What do you think? With the help of a few patrons, you might perhaps get yourself appointed governor of the new colony!"

"Mock, if it amuses you, but we're still entitled to hope that unexpected things await us; on my part, it's more than a presentiment—it's almost a conviction..."

"One can ask no more than to believe in the reality of what one desires."

"Who knows? A new country, with its own flora and fauna," I added, without taking any notice of Ceintras' interruption.

"It's impossible to imagine life in this region of cruel cold and hopelessness—and I'm curious to know on what your conviction is founded?"

"On many things, especially the legends that circulate among the tribes living near the Pole. Do you know that the Eskimos of Greenland speak freely of fabulous lands situated in the far North, beyond the ice? It's necessary to give credence to legends, which are not lies but translations of the truth; it's very rare that they don't correspond to something, and these are told about the Pole…"

"Have evidently not been recounted by anyone who has been there to see. At any rate, if events really do turn out to confirm these legends, it will only remain for me to offer you my condolences, for, evidently, you will have been beaten to it—you will not be the first tourist to have visited the region, and the ground will have been cut from under your feet in the most vexatious manner possible. In the final analysis, therefore, you will have cause to rejoice if, as there is every reason to believe, the immediate surroundings of the Pole are in no way different from the terrain over which we are traveling."

"Nevertheless," I hazarded, running out of arguments, "the open sea…"

"Oh, nonsense! The open sea! Even if we see it, people are so tired of hearing about it that it won't be anything new…"

He interrupted himself suddenly and cocked an ear; the explosions of the engine had suddenly become irregular. He muffled himself in furs and went out on to the walkway.

The cause of the malfunction was quickly discovered: an electrical wire that had subsided against a cylinder had been damaged by the heat. In order to facilitate the repair, Ceintras stopped the engine briefly. Then we noticed that, although the propellers were motionless, the ground was nevertheless fleeing beneath us at great speed.

"Damn!" cried Ceintras. "The air currents I expected to encounter are becoming increasingly powerful. We'll get considerably ahead of our timetable."

"But what about coming back?" I asked, anxiously.

"Well," my companion replied, calmly, "if the struggle against the wind is too difficult, instead of retracing our route we'll continue straight ahead."

He set the engine going again, engaged the propellers and accelerated to top speed.

Then he suggested uncorking the champagne. I consented readily. Everything was going marvelously and steering involved little more than keeping the balloon pointed in the right direction. When we had both emptied our bottles, the conversation became very animated, although neither of us was taking much notice of the meaning of the other's words. We were carried away by our obsessions as irresistibly as the balloon was by its own power and that of the wind.

"Glory," said Ceintras. "Immortality. Christopher Columbus, all over again..."

"Things," I replied, "that no man would have been able to imagine..."

"Enthusiastic reception, universal reputation..."

"New points of view, a scientific revolution..."

My dreams seemed decidedly more utopian than his, however, and I began to realize that I had only expressed them so strongly in order to delude myself, and to retain a desperate confidence until the last possible moment.

In order to get rid of the bottles that we had just drunk, I lifted the hatch of an opening lodged in the floor of the cabin—and was struck dumb. Our speed had increased further and the ground no longer appeared, in that narrow frame, as anything but a flat grey surface over which thin dark lines ran.

"Come and see," I said. "The wind has got the bit in its teeth. What does that signify?"

Ceintras interrupted his hymn of praise in his own honor to look for himself, and leaned over the aperture in his turn. He stood up, stupefied and—it immediately seemed to me—rather disappointed.

"Are we in danger?" I asked him.

"Danger? No—but in truth..."

"What? Spit it out, then?"

"Very well. Here it is: it could be...it could be, after all, that it is your expectations that are justified, at least partially...for this unexpectedly violent and sudden wind can only be caused by an abrupt difference in temperature between the place where we are and the one we're heading for."

This time, however, I did not have long to take advantage of the unexpected authorization that Ceintras had given me to pursue my dreams. My companion, who had left me to go into the warming-room, reappeared almost immediately, very pale, and said: "Take a look!"

I went forward and I looked. He had opened the two large forward portholes. An immense violet light was visible on the horizon—and we were heading straight towards it!

V. The Violet Daylight

Death is merely the most unintelligible of enigmas and what terrifies us most of all therein is the unknown. It seems that the fear of death and the horror of not knowing, of not understanding, are two closely kindred sentiments, and that it is correct to label the anguish that grips us in the face of an unknowable fact "the shudder of the little death." I do not think I have ever experienced that sentiment more acutely than in the first minutes that followed the appearance of the light. So it was that, having ardently wished for prodigies. I trembled at their approach.

Hands clenched upon the balustrade of the walkway, I felt beads of sweat on my temples despite the frightful biting cold against which, in my emotion and my haste, I had taken scant care to protect myself. Meanwhile, as we advanced towards it, the light gradually extended itself across the horizon. As time went by, we were able to take account of what there was about it that was strange—or, to put it better, "never seen before." To human eyes, the fire of the Sun appears as a calm and serene radiation of uniform brightness. By contrast, this light was not motionless; one might have taken it for the reflection in the sky of an immense invisible torch, which vacillated from moment to moment. At other times, large undulations ran across it from one end to the other, parallel to the ground and it then resembled a vast immaterial and sparkling flag whose fabric as rippling in the wind.

"What *is* that?" I murmured, eventually, in a very faint voice.

My companion replied with a vague gesture, then said: "Perhaps an aurora borealis—a prodigious aurora borealis…or some other meteorological phenomenon that no one has had the opportunity to observe before…"

He did not appear to find this explanation very satisfactory himself, though; his physiognomy expressed both anxiety and irritation. Doubtless in order to permit his perspicacity to triumph over mine on at least one point, he added: "In any case, my anticipations regarding a more clement temperature were correct. Look at the thermometer…"

That did not interest me, however. I felt as if I were on the edge of a precipice, tottering in the grip of vertigo. In order to prevent me from fainting, I needed Ceintras to furnish me— by way of a branch to which I might cling—with a rational explanation of the strange phenomenon. I interrupted him, and in the pleading tone of a man condemned to death, whose appeal has already been rejected and who no longer has the shadow of a hope, I said: "But that light—that light?"

"Wait a while," he replied, with some impatience. "We're getting there; we'll be able to see…"

Without noticing it, we had achieved a rather elevated altitude, the relative warmth of the atmosphere that surrounded us having been caused by a progressive expansion of the hydrogen. We could see that the white and grey snow about 500 meters in front of us then acquired a violet tint; the line of demarcation between the pale polar light through which we were still moving and the zone of surprising luminosity seemed very neat, like that which separates the part of a street directly illuminated by oblique sunlight from the part on which the shadow of the houses falls.

A minute later, we were on the very threshold of the mystery.

How can I describe the first impression I received of that landscape? Have you ever placed a piece of stained glass before your eyes? Even when the Sun is shining with all its brilliance, one would think that the horizon has diminished, that the sky has become heavier and drawn closer to the Earth; the illuminated parts take on a livid aspect and the smallest shadowed corner becomes the repair of fear. When I was very young, playing in the vestibule of the château, I sometimes amused myself by looking at the garden through a door in which panes of variously-colored glass were framed and imagining that I was entering another world, or that the sky had taken on that tint permanently. When I succeeded in persuading myself of that, there was a horrible sensation of oppression and sadness. The atmosphere suddenly seemed to become unbreathable; I dared not move, for it seemed to me that the air, in becoming less clear, had also become less fluid, and that the slightest movement would be as painful as carrying a heavy burden. For as long and as well as I could, I consolidated the illusion in order to increase my anguish, until the moment when, with my nerves taut and my throat constricted, ready to burst into tears, I suddenly opened the door. Then I recklessly filled my eyes again with the limpid and familiar azure; I ran out; I took a deep breath; it was the end of the nightmare, a marvelous liberation...

Now, I found myself in almost the same state of mind as when, in the days of my childhood, I had looked at the grounds for a long time through the violet pane—but this time, it was impossible for me to open the door.

Because we still had snow beneath us, its reflected light on our faces and the surrounding objects slightly attenuated the fantastic character given to them by that light, which was dazzling and somber at the same time. But the temperature continued to rise and glimpses of the ground showed through here and there. A few more minutes went by, and the last vestiges of snow soon vanished completely before our eyes. The thermometer measured six degrees Centigrade; surprised by this abrupt warmth, we were streaming with sweat. We were also overwhelmed by fatigue and emotion, anxiously waiting to see what would happen next.

Vegetation soon became vaguely manifest. So far as we could judge at first—for our eyes had difficulty doing their work in that unaccustomed light—the plants must have belonged to different species of tree-ferns and cacti, and did not grow to more than a meter high. The ground was covered with short dense grass, which extended without interruption as far as the eye could see. The landscape no longer had anything authentically terrestrial about it. That became more obvious when the mantle of fog that covered the horizon suddenly lifted and the polar Sun appeared on the far side of the plain, like an immense shield of polished metal. The power of the master of the world seemed to be annihilated here by a singular luminous force that had invaded the sky; no radiation emanated from it, and in that violet light it was like a glow-worm within the glare of an arc-lamp.

Then, for the first time, we heard close by the sound of the air whipped by invisible wings. A little shadow passed very close to us with a strident screech and collided with the roof of the cabin. Our eyes tried to follow it, but, within a second, the thing had already disappeared.

"It's terrible!" sobbed Ceintras.

He turned towards me. Tears were beginning to flow from beneath his swollen eyelids, gleaming blue and yellow like drops of decay. The Polar light confused the features of his terror-ravaged face, exaggerating the wrinkles and tumefying the lips. He gave the frightening impression of a walking and talking cadaver—but I was near to tears too, and my appearance could not have been much different from his.

"My God," the poor chap murmured, drawing back as far as the walkway. "We look like dead men!"

Our hostility had taken many forms, from the basest to the most noble, since furious hatred had caused our fists to clench and made us resemble beasts—to the point of an emulation that sometimes led us to strike heroic attitudes. Seeing Ceintras so depressed and miserable, my courage was suddenly reborn.

"After all," I said, "if you were in control of your nerves at this moment, you would appreciate that nothing is threatening us. We merely have to advance prudently into this unknown world. If need be, a turn of the rudder will quickly get us out of trouble."

"Certainly, certainly," he stammered—and he was shaken from top to toe by a sudden frisson. Again, the screech resounded in our ears, immediately followed by others. This time we had time to see one of the creatures silhouetted in black against the violet background of the sky. It seemed to be a sort of bat, flying vertically, and furnished with a kind of beak, very long and very thick.

"Well, Ceintras, were my presentiments mistaken? Are we not confronted by a new flora and fauna? Come on, don't be so downcast! It's better for you that things have turned out this way—it can only add to your glory! Our story will interest the public much more than if we had found nothing unexpected at the end of our journey. Think of the swarms of journalists that will be hammering on your door when we return—but don't let that stop you attending to your controls."

My words reassured him somewhat. He came back into the warming room and, as we were nearing the ground, manifested the intention of opening the hot air tap. I stopped him.

"We have to land here," I said to him.

"You're mad! Don't even think about it!" he exclaimed, looking at me with eyes dilated by fear.

"It seems to me to be indispensable, though," I insisted, "to collect a few specimens of minerals, plants, and even—if possible—animals. Let me pass; I want to load my rifle."

He did not want to listen. He said that he would rather blow up the balloon than yield to my crazy desire. Then he calmed down, suggesting to me that had plenty of time, and that it would be better to put off the excursion until later. As that seemed fair enough, all things considered, I gave in, and we continued on our way at an altitude of about 400 feet.

The terrain had not changed, except that the elements of the vegetation now appeared larger and taller. What struck me about their appearance was that, unlike the majority of terrestrial plants, they increased more in breadth than height. One might have thought that some invisible obstacle was preventing them from growing above a certain limit, or that the ground attracted their branches more than the sky.

Shortly afterwards, an accumulation of white vapor signaled the presence of water to us. A few minutes later, we glimpsed a river beneath these vapors, like a burnished silver blade that some giant had left behind in the middle of the plain.

"Look!" Ceintras suddenly said to me. "The temperature down there must be getting lower again; I can see patches of snow on the ground."

I leaned over the balustrade and fixed my eyes in the direction in which Ceintras was pointing.

"Ceintras!"

"What is it?"

"Come and see—it's as if the snow were moving."

Each snowy white fragment did indeed seem to be moving and varying its contours, as a flock of sheep might have done as some of them drew closer or more distant from others.

"It's frightful," my companion murmured, ready to faint.

"No," I replied, "it's strange, at the most. We're apparently in the presence of an optical phenomenon due to a visual milieu that is new to us...or we're the victims of a hallucination."

"Yes, yes," he repeated, mechanically, "a hallucination. Nevertheless..." He rubbed his eyes and leaned downward s desperately. "A hallucination—that's not possible! It's moving. Look, look! And we aren't mad!"

"Then we have to go down and see what it is."

We were at the point at which, whatever might happen, it was better to risk everything than remain any longer in the pangs of indecision; this time, undoubtedly, Ceintras would be easily swayed by my desire. At the same moment, though, the violet light diminished and a sort of twilight soon descended, furrowed with reflections and fluorescences. Gradually, we fell back into the half-light through which we had been traveling since leaving Franz-Josef Land. I realized then that the somber light of the Pole had already become necessary to us, and that, abruptly deprived of it, we were going to lose the use of our eyes for a while.

The atmosphere was crackling around us, electrical sparks appearing periodically, like those that our magneto produced in the engine's cylinders to ignite the gas. The stars beyond seemed motionless and distant. The snow beneath us still seemed to be stirring vaguely. The cries of the large bats were no longer resounding in our ears, and yet the air was not absolutely silent; with a little attention, we could perceive a soft susurrus and muted whistling sounds that seemed to be coming all the way from the surface of the ground.

"This is beyond comprehension," said Ceintras, whose excess of fear gave him a semblance of energy for a few minutes. "We have to go. We have to get out of here as quickly as possible!"

In spite of my desire to be, or to appear to be, the stronger of the two of us, I felt incapable of offering him the least resistance just then. In truth, the indescribable horror of the spectacle excused that pusillanimity. While I studied my companion's face and the somber reflection of my own in the cabin's porthole, I had the impression once again that we were dead, that nothing remained of us but two cadavers impelled by an irresistible force, not towards oblivion and rest but towards an inferno populated by ghosts, specters and nameless things that I thought I could already sense swarming beneath us—for, at intervals, slow greenish undulations ran through the last vestiges of the violet light; under that coloration the ground, and the vague white patches moving thereupon, acquired the appearance of an immense charnel-house over which a dubious moonlight spread.

"Let's go, then!" I exclaimed, in an unsteady voice. "We'll figure out later what's the best thing to do."

"Yes, yes! Go...we have to go," said Ceintras, breathlessly. "You can see it—this is the country of madness and death!"

Knocking over everything that got in his way, he raged feverishly against the sky, studded with pale stars. "Go...we have to go," he repeated.

He accelerated to top speed—and, to get us away from the ground as soon as possible, he opened a canister of hydrogen and the hot air tap at the same time...

A terrifying enigma presented itself then. The motor hummed madly; the little manometer that measured the interior pressure of the enveloped indicated that the pressure could not be further increased without danger—but it was all futile. We were neither advancing nor climbing; one might have thought that invisible hands and impalpable chains were preventing our progress and hauling us gradually towards the ground.

As if to bring all these emotions to a head, the most prodigious thing imaginable in such a place appeared. Mounted on a hillock and silhouetted against the sky, it was a sort of disk of grayish metal, fixed at the summit of an exceedingly long stalk, like one of those that mark the entrance to a racecourse, but much larger. There was no doubt about it: the apparatus was the work of intelligent industry—and that conclusion offered itself immediately to my mind in all its implacable clarity.

It did not have time to sink in, though; an inexplicable drowsiness overcame me, so sudden and violent that I was unable even to try to collect my will-power to oppose it. I heard, as if from a great distance, Ceintras—similarly weighted down by drowsiness—ask me, in a feeble voice: "What's happening?"

I did not have the strength to reply, and we sank into a profound unconsciousness.

VI. On the Brown Stone

It was not until much later that I could make an estimate of the duration of that lethargy. When I woke from it for the first time, it seemed as likely to have lasted a month as an hour. The events that had preceded it were so vague and so extraordinary that I could find nothing in them at first to which my present sensations and thoughts could be connected.

The only precise impression I had was that the slumber might have been further prolonged, and that it was by accident rather than by reason of my satiety that it had come to an end.

I thought of the distant dawns of my infancy, when a domestic had needed to come into my room, coming in and going out rapidly, carefully muffling the sound of his footsteps; when the silence had become absolute again, I suddenly perceived that my eyes were open...

Something analogous to that must have happened. I recall getting up with a start, and looking around fearfully. Ceintras was snoring, propped up in a corner of the warming room, with his head upright, his legs apart, his hands joined together, his mouth open and his forehead creased by a single furrow: a troubled sleep, seemingly replete with nightmares.

A flood of violet light came in through the portholes; it was "daylight."

Then there was a terrible anguish. Where were we? What had become of the balloon, left to its own devices during the possibly long interval in which its pilots had been unconscious? I opened the door...

The balloon was resting on the ground: the polar ground on which, the evening before, we had not dared to land. Suppressing my apprehension, I got down and made a tour of the machine. A cursory examination assured me that no functional unit had suffered. The engine had stopped simply for lack of petrol. The envelope seemed a trifle flaccid, but that did not matter; provided that the motor could be started again, we would only have to open the hot air tap to resume our flight.

I was about to go wake Ceintras and bring him up to date when I was struck by a fact of which I had not taken immediate notice. The balloon was resting on its shock-absorbers as stably as if it had been attached by numerous solid mooring-ropes. I noticed then that we had set down on a long rectangular brown stone, and that the shock-absorbers were irresistible stuck to it. One might have thought that they had been welded to it—and yet, given the quantity of hydrogen that was evidently still in the envelope, the ascensional force could not be much inferior to the force of inertia represented by the dead weight of the apparatus. In consequence, a slight impulse should have been sufficient to displace or lift the balloon. I tried to do that—first by hand, then using the barrel of my rifle, which I had prudently brought with me, as a lever—but it was all in vain.

After a few minutes, it seemed evident to me that the balloon's adherence to the rock and the mysterious obstacle that had hindered our progress the previous evening were intimately related. I then had the very clear impression of a hidden intelligence that had been spying on us for some time, which had caught us in a trap and was in control of us at that very moment.

We were *not alone*. Tangible and irrefutable proof, the high-set metal disk shone with a dull gleam a few meters away. Suddenly, in the dense thicket of cacti and tree-ferns, I heart a noise that made my heart leap into my throat...

I shouldered my weapon and went forward, trembling; the foliage stirred again about ten meters to my left. The gun went off, almost of its own accord!

Nothing more...

Then I perceived that my fear had created phantoms and that the shivering of the foliage had only been caused by the wind; it was increasing, coming off the ice-sheet in glacial gusts which, in the warmth of the Pole, pricked my face and hands periodically as if with brief and penetrating thrusts of a dagger.

Ceintras appeared on the walkway, drawn by the noise of the gunshot. I ran to him and told him everything that I had established since my awakening. He was content to nod his head, making no reply. He seemed quite bewildered. Then affecting the most detached and tranquil attitude in the world, I asked: "Did you sleep well?"

He seemed to have difficulty finding words. "Badly, very badly. A strange thing—I remember that I once had to undergo an operation that required the use of chloroform…"

"Well?"

"Well, last night I had the impression of a sleep analogous to that into which one falls under the influence of chloroform—a sleep that is odiously overwhelming and during which, profound as it is, you still retain a glimmer of consciousness, to take account of the fact that you're a slave…"

"It's as if you're shackled, tied down by 1000 chains; you make desperate efforts to break them, but you know that there's no alternative but to await the good will of a master…"

"That's right. And then, to cap it all, frightful nightmares descended upon me…"

"What nightmares?"

"How can I describe them? It seemed to me that I was falling slowly into some submarine abyss, in the midst of gigantic cephalopods, and that I felt their tentacles periodically brushing my skin…" He collected himself momentarily, then he said: "Perhaps I'm wrong to call it a nightmare; it bore less resemblance to something dreamed than to a real sensation perceived while semi-conscious."

I could not suppress a shudder; Ceintras' words had suddenly illuminate a vague memory within me, and at that moment I was almost certain that I had been victim only a few minutes before to a nightmare that resembled his…except that the cephalopods had been replaced by bats or vampires. The coincidence was strange, to say the least, and if the two dreams had no real component, it had to be a case of telepathy.

A more logical and more frightening conclusion imposed itself, though, in the realization that living creatures, native to this region—creatures of an intelligence and power that seemed at that moment to be prodigious—had drawn us to them by means of some unknown mechanism that exerted an enormous magnetic force. Then, desirous of observing us, they had approached us while we were asleep—a sleep that they had probably provoked artificially.

Should I let Ceintras in on the conclusion to which my inductions had led me? I felt sorry for him. He had let himself fall on to a boulder and his vague and vacillant eyes were staring through or beyond the objects at which they were directed. His attitude suggested an infinite weariness; I had the distinct impression of witnessing a frightful mental distress, and I attempted to appeal to his initiative in the hope of rousing him and restoring his self-possession.

"What do you intend to do?" I asked.

"I don't know. I'll see…"

He took a few steps towards the balloon and leapt on to the brown stone to which the shock-absorbers were stuck. I saw him lurch then, sway as if to recover his balance and fall awkwardly on his hands, without his feet having budged a centimeter. I ran to help him.

"Don't come any closer, for God's sake!" he cried, howling like an animal caught in a trap. "Don't come any closer!"

I was already on the stone, though, where I continued as I had before to be able to come and go without hindrance. Ceintras, on the other hand, was as incapable of taking a step as if his feet had been inexorably riveted to the spot.

"Are you in pain?" I said, trying in vain to free him.

"No, evidently not—but they'll come now, to take possession of me. Save yourself, as quickly as you can. Just kill me before you go, for mercy's sake—don't let me fall into their hands alive…a rifle-shot, here, between my eyes…quickly!"

"You're talking like a madman," I replied, shrugging my shoulders. Hang on—try to slip out of your shoes. I think that'll avoid my having to kill you."

He obeyed, uncomprehendingly, but his distress was the only thing that stopped him extracting himself easily from his unlaced shoes.

"Carry me!" he cried, afterwards. "Don't let me touch the ground, since their damned sorcery doesn't seem to have any effect on you…"

I burst out laughing. "You don't have to worry: the sorcery only affected your shoes, probably because their soles have iron nails."

You know Ceintras well enough by now not to find it extraordinary that the happy outcome of this adventure caused him to pass from excessive discouragement to an exaggerated and altogether untimely joy. As for his confidence in the future, which was immediately manifest in a considerable reinforcement of his gestures and the loudness of his voice, it would have roused the most depressed of mortals—provided that the mortal in question had not lived for nearly a year in close company with the poor devil.

"A magnet! They tried to trap us with the aid of a magnet! They imagined that we were unfamiliar with its properties. In fact, they must be even more frightened than us—why, otherwise, would they be hiding? Am I hiding? Am I hiding? Ah! Ah! Ah! Just let them show themselves! I'm waiting for them…I'll make sure that they won't want to play any more nasty tricks on us for a long time…"

I thought it advisable to put a slight brake on his enthusiasm. "What about the balloon? How do you plan to get it loose?"

Ceintras was untroubled by such a small matter. "The balloon? Oh, yes! Well, we'll uncouple the shock-absorbers, and pfft! The unweighted balloon will make a little jump 1000 meters into the air. When they come looking for us…they can keep the shock-absorbers as a souvenir, along with my pair of shoes! We'll be gone, never setting down again until we get back—or only setting down with extreme prudence. Damn! Let's talk about something else. I'm hungry. To your stove, cook!"

The meal was abundant, well washed-down and very cheerful. When a cause of sadness or anxiety persists any longer than 24 hours, it is inevitable that a relaxation takes effect in those subject to that sadness or fear. We set about eating, drinking and chatting with a zest that had nothing fake about it; it was in no way due to a more or less conscious desire to stupefy ourselves, but came from the utmost depths of our sincerity.

We were getting accustomed to the strange country, and we were no longer thinking, to our considerable discomfort, about the mysteries that surrounded us—and, in the violet daylight of the Pole, comfortably installed in the tree-ferns, next to the river the color of burnished silver, we uncorked the champagne with as much pleasure as we would have done on the bank of the Seine or the Oise, beneath the clear blue sky of the Ile-de-France.

Mentally and physically fortified, we resolved with one accord to go exploring.

VII. Ceintras Loses his Shadow and his Mind

We went along the river bank for about half a mile. The silence was so profound that the sound of our footsteps and the lapping of the water seemed enough to fill the sky.

What was that river? Where did it come from? Where did it go? There were so many questions that we asked one another vaguely, but which we were, alas, quite incapable of answering. When we looked behind us, the river appeared to emerge from the mist in the far distance, after many leagues of the plain, probably from the ice-sheet. In front of us, 100 meters downstream, it vanished behind a ridge of blue-tinted, steep and jagged rocks—the only unevenness that broke the monotony of the immense flatness.

As if these rocks had sheltered the plants from something that prevented them from growing freely everywhere else, the vegetation at their base became gradually more arborescent. As we approached, little birds, which had been perching in a sort of little wood, flew off with shrill chirps in the direction of the rocks, then made an abrupt turn and passed over our heads in a hectic flock. They had long beaks and blue-colored wings, and were little different from our kingfishers.

We reached the summit of the hill by means of a ramp of loose rocks that jutted out into the stream of the river; from there we could study the polar panorama. A circular fog-bank limited it in every direction, forming the diaphanous wall of an immense vase, within which the violet light was seething like a liqueur. It was diluted in an atmospheric fluid, in proportions that varied, for obscure reasons according to the time and place—for, when the wind blew with some force, one could actually see the air move. The hill, which was steep on the side at which we had arrived, sloped down gently to rejoin the plain in front of us. The river ran for some distance between high blue cliffs of clay. To our right, in a cavity in the misty wall, the dull eye of the Sun seemed to open indifferently upon the country that was not its domain. Disks like the one that I had seen on the evening when we arrived at the Pole were erected at intervals, marking out the immensity of the plain and the plateau.

Turning our backs to the river, we continued our excursion, remaining half way up the hill. Bizarre flowers with fleshy and rounded calices grew in hollows in the ground. Then, in the shelter of a rugged scree slope, we discovered a narrow cavern opening like a wound in the rocky flesh of the hillside; sharp little screeches emerged therefrom as we passed by. I stopped, hesitantly, and interrogated Ceintras with my eyes—but he, not having yet lost his impetus and his energy as yet, went forward resolutely, saying: "We must go in."

I followed him, and observed with amazement that it was as bright within the tortuously-walled tunnel as it was without; the violet light extended into it, penetrating into the smallest corners, chasing away all the shadows. The cries from the depths increased in response to the noise of our footsteps; then there was a furious flutter of wings, and animals passed over our heads, brushing them. I say "animals" because I was incapable, at first, of giving them a more precise name.

With a sudden thrust of a gun-butt, Ceintras struck down one that was still hanging from the ceiling of the cavern. It was about 20 centimeters long; its head resembled that of a snake, but the mouth was broader and larger. The wings were comprised of greenish membranes, and appeared to me to be closely analogous to those of our bats.

"It's some unknown species of fruit-bat!" I exclaimed

"No," Ceintras replied, simply, while palpating the creature.

"But the general appearance...and those wings..."

"Those wings are not the wings of a bat. Look: they're not sustained by four fingers, but only by the outermost finger, which is extremely elongated. The others only enable the creature to suspend itself. Also, the anterior limbs are larger, the head more developed, the jaw horny and equipped with a multitude of sharp teeth. Then again...it doesn't have any hair...neither hair nor feathers. In which case..."

"What?"

Without relying he rummaged in his pockets, took out a knife, opened the animal's body feverishly, exposed the heart and cut it out.

"That settles it: two auricles but only one ventricle. It's a reptile!"

"A flying reptile?"

"Certainly," he said, a trifle pale. "They existed, once..."

"When was that?"

"Millions of years ago. This one appears to belong to a species that was believed to be extinct. If my memory isn't playing me false, what I have I my hands is definitely a ptero-dactyl."

That scientific term recalled memories of my college days; I remembered the monstrous creatures of past eras whose depiction, in textbooks of paleontology, had struck my imagination so powerfully.

"That's amazing, magnificent! We have to trap some live ones and take them with us."

Ceintras had sat down on a stone. Still holding the dis-emboweled and bloody creature in his hand, he was staring straight ahead of him into the void. The sound of my words made him start.

"Take them with us? Where are we going to put them?" he asked.

"In the balloon, of course—what's extraordinary about that?"

He shook his head, made a vague gesture, and said, in a strange voice: "You can't prevent what once existed from ex-isting still," he murmured, as if talking to himself. "What has been hidden, but still exists somewhere...and sometimes you come across it, find it...but then it's you that once was, and can't get back to what is...or rather, it's so far away, so far very away that it takes centuries, and more than centuries, to get back..."

I interrupted him anxiously "What's that you're saying?"

He shivered; then his eyes lost their nebulous fixity. He stood up again, collected himself, and said pretending to laugh; "What am I saying? Things that are going through my head—stupid things! Let's not spend too long down here."

I thought that he was trying to make himself interesting, or to mock me, and it did not seem to be worth persisting. After searching vainly for more pterodactyls—they had not thought it wise to remain in the cavern, at our disposal—we went back to the exit.

Suddenly, Ceintras, who was walking slightly ahead of me, looked in every direction and cried out, with an expansive gesture of folly and despair: "My shadow! Where's my shadow?"

The question seemed so ridiculous to me that I remained bewildered for a moment, incapable of making any reply. Then, looking down at the ground, I perceived that neither Ceintras' shadow nor my own was projected anywhere. Objects were as bright on top as underneath, on the right and on the left.

Until then, we had not noticed that absolute absence of shadows, which, even more than the coloration of the light diffused in the atmosphere, gave the landscape its dream-like character, its seeming impossibility—or its hallucinatory strangeness, at the very least.

Ceintras was still howling "My shadow! Where's my shadow?" while turning round and round.

I thought that he was still joking; to put an end to the tiresome comedy, I said: "That's enough! Given that this light isn't coming from any precise source, and that it's a property of the air in this part of the world, it's quite natural that it should be everywhere, like the air, and that there are no shadows anywhere."

He lowered his head like a child caught doing something naughty, and, after collecting himself momentarily, replied in a tone of almost shameful humility: "Don't pay any attention…something came over me in that cave; I've got a headache and it's very hard to think...almost as hard as it is to move."

"The fact is," I admitted, "that I too seem to have limbs of lead."

After we had taken a few steps, that impression of heaviness relented slightly. We went back to the river and went down to the bank, at the foot of the hill. Then Ceintras knelt down, leaned over the water like an animal, and drank deeply.

"It's water, all the same," he said, as he got up. "Except that it doesn't make a good mirror—our faces look frightful."

When I asked him how he was feeling, he replied: "Much better—but it's a long way from here to the balloon, and I'm still a bit tired. Do you want to stop for a little while?"

We sat down side by side, our feet dangling over the water. For some time, we were absorbed in our own thoughts.

"You know," I eventually said to Ceintras, who seem to be deep in thought, with his head in his hands, "this landscape reminds me of those I drew when I was a boy to distract myself; everything in my paintings was flat, and in the same plane, because I didn't know how to use shading."

"Yes," he replied. "It's only by means of shadow that we can perceive relief. I remember now that, a little while ago, we only discovered the hill once we were at its base. We can only distinguish differences of color within this landscape, and that's disturbing...it's difficult for us to take account of it. Also, we have no notion of it...this damned light that comes from everywhere!"

After 20 more minutes of silence, Ceintras continued: "There's an impression that I can't shake off; as I consider our surroundings, I can't help thinking of them as something artificial, *fake*; this light reminds me of the light with which theater technicians bathe certain scenes of enchantment. Here too there must be technicians, with enormous magnetic or electrical forces at their disposal: masters of a fluid that can render the air luminous and warm it up to a benign temperature. Except, you see, that they're totally lacking in aesthetic sensibility! They too have no idea how to use shading! It's annoying, even tiresome…very tiresome…"

"Are you in pain?" I asked him, troubled by his apparent lassitude.

"No," he said. "It's just that, as I already told you, this light cramps my thoughts. It seems to penetrate into me, disintegrating and scattering all my ideas; I have to make an effort to hold them together. And yet I'd like to be able to think—I need to think, to discover what *they* are."

He became animated, and soon became so voluble that it was impossible for me to get a word in. "Yes, what are they? How can they hide so well? Not a house, not a building…and yet they indubitably exist: those metal disks, the mysterious entrapment of our balloon…do you think they might be invisible?"

I shrugged my shoulders. He got up, took a few steps along the river bank, and suddenly let out a cry: "Come and see—a door!"

I ran. Ceintras pointed his finger at a metal panel framed in an indentation in the rocky cliff. Dazedly and mechanically, I rapped three times on the panel; the echoes of the sound seemed to reverberate to infinity in the depths of the Earth.

"It's hollow," I said, lowering my voice instinctively.

"A door! It's a door!" cried Ceintras. "They must live underground. That's why we don't see them anywhere!"

"Should we go in?" I proposed.

"Damn it!" he said, recoiling slightly. "That seems a trifle reckless."

"I don't deny it," I replied. "These polar folk are intelligent and civilized, though—they must be rational creatures to fashion metals, make use of the forces of nature…and rational creatures, as they are and we are, must always understand one another in the end."

"But…"

"Let me speak. No hesitation is possible. Our balloon is nailed to the ground by their will. It will be necessary, sooner or later—and the sooner the better—to meet them, even though they're avoiding us…to have dealings with them, to make ourselves understood, to obtain our freedom. That's the best course of conduct to follow—and, if you want to know what I think, it's our only hope of getting out of here."

"All right, I'll follow you," Ceintras said, after a few moments of reflection. "But first we have to open the door."

"That won't be difficult. I can't see any catch or lock; they must have no fear of thieves in these parts!"

Despite all our efforts, though, the door would not open. It was irresistibly stuck within its metal frame. This time, instructed by our previous experience, we understood soon enough what the reason was; the people of the Pole used magnetic currents instead of locks and keys!

"What do you expect?" said Ceintras, who had tried with all his might to open the door as soon as he had realized that it was impossible. "What do you expect? We'll have to put off the execution of your plan until later!"

He did not appear to be particularly upset. He sat down, then got up again, took a few steps while whistling, then finally lay down at full length, face down, in front of the door. Meanwhile, sitting a few feet away, I formulated various plans, ingenious and audacious but a trifle vague. It was necessary to get hold of one of these people who were disagreeably insistent on having us as guests, and hold him hostage, in order to oblige the others to give in to our demands. How we were to contrive to get our hands on him was a question I judged it superfluous to go into at present…

A further exclamation from Ceintras brought me back me from these reveries. "These impressions—look at these impressions in the clay!"

"They're everywhere," I said, bending down. "How does it come about that we didn't see them before?"

"Doubtless because of this light, this accursed light," Ceintras growled.

The moist and flexible clay has clearly retained the tracks of an animal's feet. Here and there grooves could also be seen, like those left behind by trailing tails. Further away, in a muddy smear, there was a partial impression of the body of one of these creatures, which had fallen down there, or laid itself down at full length.

"What can it be?" I asked Ceintras.

"One foot here, the other there," he said, looking attentively at the ground. "This has all the appearance of a biped's track—or rather, an animal that only uses its hind limbs and its tail to walk, something like a kangaroo. This imprint in the shape of an ivy-leaf, however...I seem to recall...wait! Yes! It's quite similar, although smaller, to the fossil imprints we possess of the iguanodon..."

"The iguanodon?"

"Yes, another monster of ancient eras. In coming here, we've taken a great leap into the past. Relics of the Cretaceous period are still alive hereabouts: ancient species have been perpetuated here for millions of years!"

"But, since life here seems to have followed a course different from anywhere else," I said, "will not the human species itself conform to that general law? Who can tell whether we might be separated from these polar humans by an infinitely deep gulf?"

"Yes, perhaps...perhaps they have, indeed, evolved in a different fashion, and there are a few differences between them and us. They live underground; they must be small, smaller than you and me, deformed and ugly. I can imagine them having the features of the gnomes of legend, like industrious and skillful dwarfs, working metals marvelously and constructing unusual machines in the depths of their tunnels. Who can tell what prodigies the ground beneath our feet conceals?"

"But what are these animal tracks in front of the door of their dwelling?"

"A herd of livestock, which, their pasturage concluded, will go back into the caverns with them."

"A herd of iguanodons—of domesticated iguanodons? What would the story of the journey be worth...if we were sure of ever returning to tell it. Except that, although I've searched hard, I can't see any imprint of a human foot among the others..."

"This opening is doubtless that of the cowsheds, and, as the animals are domesticated, they must return to the fold of their own accord, by force of habit..."

"Or in response to a summons called out to them..."

"Could be. After all, though, I don't know anything, and you can make these inductions as well as I can. As for the inhabitants of the Pole, they may be no more different from us than a Redskin or an Eskimo."

"How do you explain, then, that they aren't showing themselves? What if they're hatching some terrible plot against us, underground?"

"That's hardly probable. They're more likely to be frightened by these visitors that have descended from the sky."

"And the sky is so inclement overhead that they can't expect anything good to come from it. If humans have got into the habit of lodging their most cherished hopes there, it's because it's where light and heat come from, but here...!"

"Certainly. And, as I've already said, we're doubtless much taller than they are. Who knows? Perhaps they'll worship us as powerful and fearsome gods..."

In statements like these, I found my true Ceintras again—but when the hour seemed to have come to return to the balloon and we had to start walking again, incomprehensible bizarreries slid by degrees into the least of his speeches, especially at moments when, after having spoken again of a "formidable leap into the past, millions of years," he began to launch into nebulous and interminable theories regarding the past and the present, about that which had been and that which was...

In the end, I was quite unable to understand his discourse. I put it down to my fatigue.

We finally got back to the balloon. A frightful surprise awaited us there: the fundamental parts of the engine had been unbolted with a marvelous dexterity and taken away...

Ceintras looked at me, looked at the empty place, tottered, and stood still for a minute without speaking. Then, quite calmly, he shrugged his shoulders and said: "That's of no importance."

"But how do you expect to get back, now, damn it?"

"We'll go back on foot. Or, if you're afraid of getting tired as we walk, I'll fabricate a sled...and I'll hitch iguanodons to it. Well? What do you think? It will be splendid, that return?"

He hopped from one foot to the other, his hands in his pockets, looking straight ahead and beaming smugly. I saw no point in replying. This time, I understood...

VIII. The Face Haloed by Stars

Lying on the bed at the back of the cabin, Ceintras sang for a long time, paying no more attention to my presence than if I had not existed. Then, his monotonous chant became punctuated by longer and longer silences; his voice grew weaker and slower, his eyelids fluttered. Eventually, I judged by the noisy regularity of his breathing that he was asleep.

Then the horror of my situation appeared to me with a pitiless clarity. Separated from the human fatherland by in-surmountable obstacles; exiled, almost without hope of return, in a land of nightmare; condemned to the perpetual disquieting presence of a mysterious people, resourceful and probably hostile; exposed to their incomprehensible ambushes; I was also deprived, now that my companion had descended into insanity, of the only person on whom I might have been able to rely for support.

And the polar night had returned! Soon, the violet light would disappear, and there would be a futile struggle against irresistible sleep. Was I destined to wake up, this time? If it were true that the inhabitants of the Pole were afraid of us, would they not take advantage of our helplessness to kill us, or—an even more horrible hypothesis—to tie us up us and take us into the depths of their subterranean dwellings. What torture would await us there? Such were my thoughts, at the time. I surrendered myself to bleak discouragement and soon felt large tears running down my cheeks.

My nerves, deranged by so many successive emotions, were at the end of their tether. I was weak with fatigue, per-haps also with hunger, and I suddenly realized that I was about to faint. Then, utilizing all my remaining strength, I staggered to my feet and poured myself a large glass of cognac, which I drank in a single draught.

Immediately, my blood started flowing though my veins with more warmth and vivacity. "It's the only way to recover a little courage," I thought. And I drank two more glassfuls, one after the other.

Afterwards, it appeared that my fate was not as atrocious as I had imagined at first. Under the stimulant effect of the alcohol, new and more optimistic thoughts enlightened the confusion of my mind, and the crisis of despair that I had just come through seemed to be no more than the consequence of some cerebral disturbance or physical weakness. The disappearance of the engine? Well, assuming that the cruelty of men was not proportional to their power, it was probable that the people of the Pole would consent to restore it to us sooner or later. Given my feeble knowledge of mechanics, it would undoubtedly be difficult for me to get the balloon into a condition in which it would fly and steer properly, but was Ceintras' madness conclusive? I recalled that there had been times when I had considered myself slightly unbalanced, and there had certainly been much in recent events that might disturb and disorientate the sanest of minds...

Finally, supposing that it would not be impossible for me to leave this country—even if I must die here before my time—was it, after all, worth getting immeasurably depressed about it? Was there any real reason for me to be determined to return one day to my homeland, to live in the bosom of a familiar civilization again? Had I ever experienced anything there but tedium, discouragement and disgust? Better, all things considered, to enjoy the pleasure of having my only wish granted, without any afterthought, and to confront the adventure as a man with nothing to lose.

Meanwhile, waves of green iridescence were beginning to appear in the violet mantle of the polar day. Soon they were furrowing the horizon horizontally, increasingly extensive and increasingly numerous; the impending dusk transformed itself into night with incredible rapidity. Already, as on the previous evening, I felt a sort of vertigo taking hold of me, a veil descending upon my mind. My eyelids fluttered.

"No, not that! Not that!" I cried, as if I were dealing with sentient enemies...and, realizing that I was again being enslaved by fear, I started drinking again, waiting for the night...

It came, and, as I crouched in the remotest corner of the cabin, it seemed to me that it came upon me as a hunter's club strikes down a hunted beast. My limbs grew heavy; the least movement seemed to require an enormous effort of strength and will—but to my great surprise, my brain remained lucid and, from that moment on, I had a presentiment that the magnetic sleep would not take complete possession of me. Had it less purchase on my nerves, which had already been subject to it once? Was it a fortunate consequence of the alcohol I had absorbed? The two explanations presented themselves to my mind, but, for the moment, I judged it superfluous to give preference to either one of them.

I was warm, and the air in the hermetically sealed cabin had become depleted. I opened the porthole; a gust of fresh air came in from outside; the slight choking sensation that had constricted my throat all day soon disappeared. My lungs dilated more freely and I breathed the air delightedly—air that, in losing its coloration, had regained its light and fluid purity. For the first time, the landscape of the Pole was displayed to me lit only by a vague and distant sunlight. Although my eyes were confused by the abrupt variation of light and the sight of the stars during the polar day—in the usual human sense of the word—I found myself back on Earth; I was at home. Beneath the hammock in which I went to lie down, Ceintras was sleeping peacefully and profoundly. For a moment, I could almost believe that I had dreamed everything that had happened since our arrival at the Pole.

In front of me, the porthole framed a lovely circle of pale light encrusted with points of gold. My eyes turned towards it and remained fixed on the tremulous light of the stars. I understood that I was falling asleep but, at that moment, it no longer frightened me; it was by consent and not submission. My thoughts became nebulous, I asked myself what corner of space, at that point in time, I might be looking at...then I was no longer thinking at all.

Suddenly, something white appeared in the frame of the porthole. From the depths of my somnolence, I observed that it resembled a face roughly sculpted in snow, which stood out clearly against the grayish blue of the sky, surrounded by an indecisive halo of stars.

I must have remained thus for several seconds, half-conscious, looking at the thing vaguely, without attaching any more importance to it than to one of those baroque visions that often precede sleep. Then, with an abrupt flash of reason, I started and sat up, opening my eyes wide. The porthole no longer framed anything but the illimitable sky and the distant stars.

I leapt out of the hammock without fully understanding what had happened or what I was doing. My gaze wandered over the sleeping Ceintras and the half-empty bottle of cognac, and I gradually recovered a complete sense of reality. "I must have been asleep, and had a dream," I thought. But I repeated the words in vain; I could not fully convince myself.

I resolved to struggle energetically against fatigue, in order to take account of what had happened. I assured myself that my revolver was loaded, put it down beside me on a shelf, and lit a cigar. Minutes as long as centuries went by, while I waited anxiously. I saw nothing.

Eventually, I seemed to hear a slight noise outside. I took two steps, stopped...

Absolute silence had fallen again. Then, having returned my eyes to the porthole, I saw the face that was spying on me.

I saw it—or, rather, glimpsed it fleetingly—for a split second. That time was sufficient, however, for me to experience the most intense impression of horror. How can I describe it? How can I find the words to make myself understood?

Imagine the effect that might be produced by something impossible...but quasi-tangible at the same time. This time, I had not been dreaming; I was sure of it. I had seen, really seen, that creature's face: a prominent forehead, surmounted by folds of wrinkled skin, which hung down on each side like locks of snowy hair; no chin; the mouth of a reptile, with rounded nostrils at the end of a sort of pug-nose; and above that nose, eyes—large, profound eyes, which gave that monstrosity an odious semblance of humanity!

I had seen it, but I wanted to see it again, more clearly—and that feverish curiosity was stronger than the terror and the disgust. Confused noises became audible again, like whispering behind the door. Then, without further consideration of the consequences of my action, I opened it violently. There was a shock, stifled cries, leaping about, a hectic stampede...

I looked out. The thickets of cacti and tree-ferns were shaking as invisible beings fled through them.

I launched myself in pursuit of them. Momentarily, I perceived two or three white forms in a patch of open ground on the river's edge. I hastened my run, but when I arrived in the clearing there was nothing there—nothing but a door fitted into the side of the bank, exactly like the one that Ceintras and I had discovered on the preceding day.

This time, though, the door was open. Kneeling on the ground, on the very threshold of the dark tunnel, I tried in vain to see something within; there was nothing in front of me but shadow and silence. Then I heard a faint noise, analogous to the tick-tock of a pendulum clock—except, I realized, that it must actually be quite loud and coming from a long way off. I cocked my ear for a little while longer, but the door suddenly closed again, automatically, with a slam that was multiplied by distant echoes.

I consulted my watch. It had stopped during out first sleep, but I had since rewound it, in order that it would at least inform us of the duration of time, if not the hour of human-reckoned time. I established thus that the violet light had only disappeared three hours ago; the "night" would undoubtedly last for a long time yet.

Anxious about what might happen at the balloon during my absence, I slowly retraced my steps. Beneath the squat and bushy plants, in every corner where shadows amassed, I imagined creatures watching me. On several occasions, I even heard the sound of leaves rustling behind me, but when I turned around abruptly, parted the branches, searched the bushes with my hands and my eyes, or launched myself at a run along an imaginary trail, it was impossible for me to catch a glimpse of any more of the vague white shapes that I had seen a few minutes earlier.

I was streaming with sweat. Rage and exasperation were tensing my nerves painfully. I went back to the river, to drink and bathe my face. Then, for the first time, I was confronted by the most prodigious spectacle that any man had ever been able to contemplate.

On the sandy bed of the river, beneath the dark transparency of the water, phosphorescent violet gleams showed here and there, which gradually extended, also covering beds of gravel and little rocks garlanded with aquatic plants. Soon, the river assumed the appearance of running over illuminated amethysts, against which I saw, outlined in black, the silhouettes of large fish, which swam away...

Slowly, the violet light in the water was augmented, mixing with it. When it had reached the surface, the river, in the Pole's half-light, resembled some Phlegethon or Cocytus streaming with burning sulfur. After having invaded the water, though, the light climbed into the air and expanded over the banks; it was as if the river had suddenly overflowed.

Instinctively, I recoiled, placing myself on a little knoll. The light reached my feet in less than five minutes. The tranquil regularity of its ascent and diffusion gave the impression of an irresistible and fatal force. Already, in the lowest-lying parts of the plain, the Earth was inundated by it; it rose up from the ground like a vegetation of light; slender and palpitant shoots surge forth, multiplied, drew closer to one another and finally fused into an immobile sheet of light.

I repeated to myself: "It's the daylight; it's the polar daylight dawning..." And yet, I was afflicted by an anguish against with my reason could do nothing. I had the illusion of drowning, of being submerged by an immense tide; I remained motionless, clenching my fists. The light passed my shoulders, brushed my chin; then, it became horrible, for it seemed to me that, within a few seconds, I would suffocate, asphyxiate when I opened my mouth to draw breath...

However puerile or crazy it might seem, I crouched down abruptly, rather like a bather who plunges into the water all at once, in order that the disagreeable sensation of cold might last the least possible time. When I got up again, my eyes were still above the sheet of light; the upper parts of the balloon, to my left, and the hill, to my right, were the only things that still remained in the half-light, and—something that people will find difficult to imagine—as the blue of the sky became darker, the stars faded; they were completely extinguished behind the violet curtain.

I lifted my arms, and my hands, exiting from the luminous atmosphere, seemed to stand out against the sky.

A short time afterwards, I sat down to rest for a moment before continuing on my way. I remember attempting, momentarily, to bring some order to the thousands of images and confused ideas whirling in my head. I soon gave up; my strength had run out; I was exhausted.

Suddenly, the world around me seemed literally to collapse into darkness; it is impossible for me to tell now whether I had fallen asleep or fainted.

IX. Hours of Waiting

The interval that followed was painful and disturbed. Before anything definite became manifest, the violet light was extinguished and reappeared nine times over. Human sensations were blunted so swiftly that I now began to wait for the polar day, throughout the anxious nights, with veritable impatience. I divined that the nights were haunted by sly presences, but I could not see them clearly; in the hours when, covered once again by its violet mantle, the country became peaceful and deserted, I began to ask myself whether the nocturnal visions were real, or whether my over-excited brain had imaged them.

It would have been a great relief to me to share my impressions and discoveries with Ceintras. He sometimes recovered his reason, and it seemed to me that every day improved the sensibility of his mental state, but I dreaded that I might set him back or check the recovery of which it was necessary not to give up hope by excessively troubling revelations.

I viewed the approach of the night that followed the one through which I had stayed awake without too much apprehension. Because I had avoided the magnetic sleep once, I thought that I was permanently liberated from it. It was in the midst of that fine confidence that it took brutal hold of me; I did not even have time to struggle, and the terrifying dreams began again.

When I woke up, Ceintras was sitting on the ground in front of the cabin door, with his heads in his hands, sobbing.

"Why are you crying?" I asked him.

He did not seem to hear me and did not stop wailing. Then, slowly parting his fingers in front of his face, I repeated my question with greater emphasis.

"Come on, Ceintras, why are you crying?"

He was afflicted by a brief shudder, and then his wandering gaze, having strayed in various directions, met mine.

"Why am I crying? Why? Well, I thought that my troubles were over, that I could sleep peacefully. I slept so well the other night! And then—now *they*'ve come back!"

"Who are *they*?" I asked, forcing myself to hide my anxiety.

"*Them*! I don't know what to call them, you know...but I sense them distinctly. They lean over me, feel me, turn me over, sniff me—and I'm like a thing, a poor thing that can't defend itself, or cry out..."

I tried to deflect his thoughts in another direction, but everything that he had said was concordant with what I had experienced myself! During my sleep, in fact—and I can still remember it now—I had been subject, with the most complete inertia, to the soft, cold contact of tentacles, paws, hands...

On the other hand, since Ceintras had slept peacefully on the night when I had been able to remain awake, what conclusion could be drawn from that, if not that the monsters I had glimpsed, whose restless curiosity had only been disrupted by fear, had profited from our sleep and powerlessness to come back and observe us meticulously?

But what were we to make of these monsters? Must I now resign myself to see in them the intelligence of the polar world, or were they really nothing but marvelously domesticated animals that stood erect? The latter hypothesis seemed to me to be more logical at first, perhaps because it pleased me more. In order to confirm it in my own mind—I continued, of course, to say nothing to Ceintras—I searched for proofs, saying to myself: "Nowhere, neither in the environs of the trapdoors, nor the vicinity of the balloon, have I seen the imprint of a human-shaped foot. Ceintras was right; we're dealing with herds of livestock that are put out to pasture by night."

It was, however, in vain that I attempted to banish from my mind the image of the face that I had perceived on two occasions, framed in the porthole. The obsessive idea of its almost-human gaze, illuminated by some guiding intelligence, was implacable. Despite all my efforts, I returned continually to the supposition that seemed to me the worse: "What if that were the humankind of the Pole?"

The notion then became horrible. Since the polar race, isolated from the rest of the world, had not evolved in the same way as other human races, it seemed scarcely probable that any point of intellectual or moral contact existed between them and us. If that were really the case, I could no longer entertain the hope of ever establishing a relationship with my hosts.

Given that these creatures remained hidden during the day, it was necessary for me to stay awake to clarify the mystery—but I was not even in control of my sleep! I searched desperately for the cause that had enabled me, on one occasion, to arm myself against the irresistible torpor. That had not, as I had at first imagined, accustomed me to it, since I had been forced to yield to sleep on the following night. Suddenly, with an abrupt clarity, I saw myself in the cabin again, with my eyelids already growing heavy, swilling cognac to renew my courage—and I immediately had the intuition that the alcohol had sufficed to maintain me in a state of relative lucidity.

Fortunately, the provisions of alcohol that we had were considerable. At the time of our departure, I had even thought them excessive, but Ceintras, doubtless with the sole purpose of contradicting me, had refused to concede a single bottle.

As you will imagine, I did not inform my companion of my discovery. Taking advantage of a moment when he was absent, I removed all the bottles I could find from the stores and buried them behind the balloon, after hiding a little flask in my pocket that was intended to combat the first assaults of the sleep. It was not, of course, selfishness that led me to act in that fashion but simple prudence. It was, in fact, sufficient for one of us to remain awake, and logic dictated that it ought to be the one who had not lost his mind. I should also say that Ceintras had, for some time, manifested an immoderate penchant for liquor, and that, if I had not put a stop to it, our precious provision would have been rapidly exhausted. Finally, I feared that if he, too, remained awake all night, he and his madness would be a hindrance to the observations I had to make.

After our meal on the day when the bottles were placed in safe-keeping, Ceintras did not neglect to demand the ration that I usually permitted him. I had prepared a little comedy in advance, designed to fool him. In the most natural manner in the world, I went to the storage-locker; having opened it, I feigned extreme amazement, and cried: "Oh! What! All the liquor has disappeared!"

He came forward, looked into the storage-locker and then fixed his eyes on me. He appeared to be examining me suspiciously. In order to dispel his suspicions, I pretended to reflect for a few minutes; then, striking my forehead, I said: "The inhabitants of the Pole must have stolen them!"

It was a bad idea. Those simple words sufficed to make my companion furious; with his fists clenched and his face red, he launched a frightful tirade of invective against the thieves. For nearly half an hour, he ran hither and yon, without it being possible for me to calm him down or restrain him, rummaging in the nearby bushes with his hands and feet. Finally, exhausted and bathed in sweat, he let himself fall to the ground and was not long in going to sleep. There was, in any case, not much time until dusk, and I already felt an infinite lassitude weighing upon my mind and body.

I tried vainly to haul Ceintras into the cabin. Then, using what strength remained to me, I went in search of the thin mattress from the bed and installed the sleeper upon it as well as I could. Then I gathered armfuls of dry tree-ferns, which I heaped up on the ground, and I lit a huge fire, designed to frighten the monsters or to prove to them that we were not asleep. It is probable that the stratagem succeeded. At any rate, I could scarcely distinguish, so distant were they, the few white forms that appeared briefly when night fell, in the direction of the river, only to disappear almost immediately.

Ceintras, when he woke up a little later, was not a little astonished to discover that he had spent the night in the open, comfortably installed on the mattress and wrapped up in blankets.

"You were sleeping so soundly," I explained, "that I hadn't the heart to disturb you. Moreover, as you can see, last night—even though we were not protected by a door—*they* thought it best to let us alone.

He thanked me effusively for the care I had taken of his person. Throwing himself into my arms, he even begged my pardon for the annoyance that the fit of temper that he had allowed to overwhelm him on the previous evening must have caused me.

The rapid succession of troubling events had, after all, been the sole cause of he unfortunate fellow's madness. In the relative calm of the days that followed, his cerebral distress gradually diminished. To eke out our provisions, with regard to the possibility of a return of which I did not yet feel entitled to despair, I began using my rifle to kill the birds with the blue plumage that we had perceived during our first exploratory expedition. I did not take long to give up that kind of hunting, though, for the game, being meager and mediocre of taste, was really not worth the powder. Ceintras had been more fortunate. He had fabricated a reasonably adequate fishing-line, with pins and thread, and went angling in the river. Primitive as his device was, he caught plenty of excellent fish.

"It's marvelous!" he cried, triumphantly, at each new catch. "I'm no longer worried about staying here: the country has abundant resources!"

This useful distraction also had the advantage of contributing a good deal to calming him down and curing him. For my part, in order to conserve my strength and to stay awake more easily during the hours of darkness, I acquired the habit of sleeping while Ceintras was fishing.

"What a prune you are," he said to me, laughing. "You're scarcely the man of the hour, are you? I wonder what would become of you if I weren't here to provide for your nourishment."

At other times, though, I saw traces of anguish and profound anxiety marked on his physiognomy. By virtue of the acuity of sensation that certain sick people acquire, he noticed 1000 little things that escaped me, but which assumed an enormous importance in his mind and got out of proportion when they became exaggerated.

Once, he woke me up abruptly. "Didn't you see? Didn't you hear?" he cried.

What had he heard or seen? I'd have given a great deal to know—but when I questioned him, he made a vague gesture while speaking in even vaguer terms. "What did I see? Oh...it's very difficult to explain, see? In fact, am I quite sure that I saw anything? No, no...certainly not—I was seeing things! Go back to sleep, don't pay any attention...excuse me..."

And he calmly threw his fishing-line back into the river.

On other occasions, he had intuitions, presentiments of the truth that filled me with an indefinable terror. One day, he said to me: "You've seen them, haven't you? You must have seen them. What are they? Frightening, isn't it?"

"No, I haven't seen them, I assure you..."

"Yes! Yes! You've seen them...and it seems to me that I see them again in your eyes when I talk to you...oh, close your eyes, I beg of you!"

On yet other occasions, in moments of perfect lucidity, he returned to the same subject, but in a more reassuring manner. "We ought, all the same, to make our preparations to meet them you know—or to go and get the engine back, since we can't get out otherwise."

"Undoubtedly—but how do we get into the tunnels?"

"We have cartridges and gunpowder. We can blow up one of their trapdoors. Yes, that's it. And as soon as possible. This uncertainty is exasperating. Tell me, what do you think they are, in the final analysis?"

On that point, even if I had thought it appropriate to tell him what I knew, I would still not have been able to be very precise. At that time, during the few hours when the Sun alone illuminated the Pole, the mysterious beings only allowed themselves to be glimpsed at a distance. Naturally, I was torn between curiosity and dread. It often occurred to me to let the fire go out and simulate sleep in order to observe the nocturnal visitors more closely; soon, I heard the branches rustling as they passed, then the noises came closer and I made out whispering sounds a few feet away; then dread became more powerful than curiosity; I got up abruptly, lit a match...and saw nothing but confused white shapes vanishing into the half-light.

I was, however, persuaded that, for better or worse, I should not delay finding out more about them. They were evidently getting gradually bolder; before long, the fire no longer intimated them so much and they appeared at the every edge of the luminous circle. On several occasions, thinking that they had, after all, never done us any harm, even when they could have killed us without any risk, I got up and went to meet them—but the least of my movements put them to flight.

On the evening of the ninth day, inexpressibly weary of my anxious ignorance, I was utterly resolved to examine them at close range and to know—finally, to know! I even went so far as to plan to shoot one with the rifle, whatever the consequences of that reckless aggression might be. I can still see myself striding along the river bank, my blood feverishly hot, repeating in a loud voice like a madman: "That's it! As soon as night falls, I'll kill one!" And I halted momentarily in front of one of the iron doors, the inexorable guardians of the mystery; my eyes searched for a bush or a hollow in the ground where I might mount an ambush...

Suddenly, I heard the grating of metal along the grooves and the dry click of the panel at the end of its course. I turned round. In the frame of the doorway, nailed to the spot by astonishment or fear, livid in the midst of the violet light that was as abundant beneath the vault of the tunnel as it was beneath the sky, the creature was standing, facing me.

X. The Creature Shows Itself

Oh, that horrible, frightful face! In truth, at the time, I waited, with my eyes fixed upon it, for it to step back or vanish, as on the previous days—but it stayed there, and every minute seemed to increase its atrocity.

All my thoughts had fled; there was nothing left in me but a dolorous and bleak stupefaction, and the impression was so forcefully engraved upon me that it still persists today, whether I am awake or asleep, whether such a creature is before my eyes or not...

No, it would take longer than the duration of a human life to become accustomed to its odious strangeness. Ah, my wish had been granted to the fullest possible extent! I had wanted to see prodigies; I had seen them; I had seen more than enough of them! Now I shall carry the image of that face within me forever—even if I return some day to live among men—haunting my nights and my days like the worst of all nightmares or the most frightful madness.

As soon as I had observed that extremely well-developed cranium, hypertrophied in places, as if swollen by an excess of brain-tissue; as soon as, more than anything else, those large eyes, lit by an interior gleam, had met mine, I understood once and for all that the creature was endowed with reason. I recall searching doggedly for some vestige of humanity, in order to diminish, to some extent, the disturbance that realization imported into my most profound intellectual habits—but the monster's appearance was in no way reminiscent of a man's. It stood crouched on its hind limbs, and obviously walked in the same fashion, using its strong tail for support. It grotesquely short arms, instead of hanging down to rest along its sides, seemed literally to spring from its breast. It had no true hands, but had very long and delicate fingers attached directly to its wrists—longer, it seemed to me, than the arms themselves, and slightly reminiscent of tentacles.

There was no trace of hair on the face, but a dull white skin that put me in mind of the flayed head of a veal-calf. The eyes were round, slightly bulbous, framed without visible eyelids in pre-eminent orbits. Instead of a nose, there were two gaping holes from which mist emerged; beneath them, there was the wide slit of a reptilian mouth, equipped with a multitude of sharp teeth, which the thin and horny lips did not quite cover. Beads of saliva were oozing from the two corners of these lips, which almost touched the mobile and minuscule ears. The chin was non-existent, or hidden beneath the flaccid folds of soft skin piled on the neck and the upper part of the torso.

Then, two white, tenuous, almost diaphanous eyelids, like those of snakes or birds, flashed back and forth, momentarily veiling the eyes...

It was no longer possible to go on seeking to delude myself; this creature and contemporary humans were not descended from the same ancestor.

I think we spent nearly five minutes—five eternal minutes—staring at one another. Then, frozen in place by horror, I remember seeing the monster's mouth open with a soft hissing sound as it took a step towards me. I don't know why, but that mouth seemed menacing, and ready to bite. My eyes closed; I was not even capable of recoiling, and I soon felt acrid and icy breath on my face. I could not have been more frightened had I seen Death creeping up on me...

When I opened my eyes again, the face was only a few centimeters from mine.

A furious anger suddenly possessed me, stronger than disgust and fear. The monster's height was slightly superior to mine and the flaccid skin of its neck hung down to the level of my teeth. In an unimaginable fit of rage, against which my reason could do nothing, I fell forward and bit it—yes, bit, as terrified beasts do. How can I describe the sensation on my lips and tongue of that compact rubbery flesh, so difficult to penetrate?

The frightened monster let out a scream, which resonated like the screech of two copper plates abruptly rubbed against one another, leapt nimbly backwards and disappeared around a bend in the tunnel.

When calm and order had gradually returned to my mind, there was nothing I could do but curse the imprudence of my impulsive action. I understood very well that, at the decisive moment when our future—and, doubtless, our lives—hung in the balance, the least of my actions took on a considerable importance, and that, suppressing my nerves, I ought to not have done anything without very careful consideration. And what had I done! The creature had evidently approached me without any hostile intent, solely—after long hesitation—to examine me more closely in broad daylight and perhaps to attempt to enter into communication with me, and I had thrown myself upon it and bitten it, like some wild beast! Would we not be running the risk henceforth of being considered by the people of the Pole as dangerous and malevolent animals?

I went back to the balloon, extremely annoyed with myself. I found Ceintras on the river bank, busy putting away his lines and preparing to leave. All day, he had been as reasonable as could be, and it did not seem to me that anything disagreeable had altered that mental state during my absence. With a certain bitterness, I thought that, after what I had just done, I scarcely had the right to consider myself any saner than him. Then, Ceintras having asked me why I seemed so pensive, I replied without hesitation: "This is why: I've seen one of the inhabitants of the Pole. I saw him at close range, as I see you at this moment..."

"Ah! What happened?"

"Well, it wasn't a human being. It was...it was..."

"What?"

"I don't know what to tell you...something like a big lizard that stood upright on its hind legs..."

"That's what it is," murmured Ceintras, after a few moments' thought.

"What?" I exclaimed. *"That's what it is*…so you've seen one of them already?"

"Yes," he replied. "And if I haven't kept you up to date, it's because I didn't think the time was ripe…"

"Why not?"

"Why not? Because—as I'm well aware—I've been ill recently, very ill…without quite seeming to be. And I've been somewhat suspicious of thoughts that might have come to me during that illness. It's over; I'm better, much better…"

"My poor friend!" I said, taking his hand affectionately. "But what do we do now?"

"I'm still thinking about that. We'll obviously run into all sorts of difficulties. Firstly, will it ever be possible for us to make ourselves understood to these creatures? Their throats must be as incapable of imitating the sounds of human languages as ours are to produce and assemble in an intelligent manner the hisses and whistling sounds that they use to express their thoughts…"

"So you also know that their language…"

"Yes."

"Since when?"

"Only just now, for certain. Three of these singular individuals suddenly appeared on the river bank, scarcely ten meters away from me. On seeing me, they stopped, and after a few moments of bewilderment or fear, they began to converse with one another, without taking their eyes off me—for they *were* conversing, there's no possible doubt about that. If I'd stayed motionless, they might perhaps have come closer…"

"But you moved, and then…tell me! Tell me!"

"What for? You know as much as I do—and it's scarcely the moment for idle chatter…"

"Yes, but what are we to do? My God, what are we to do?"

"Do they see things in the same way that we do?" Ceintras said, without seeming to have taken any notice of my last words. "They live in a society, they're intelligent—perhaps even to a degree that surpasses what is humanly imaginable...but that's no reason why their sentiments shouldn't be very different from ours. If they have no notion of pity, of clemency, what will become of us?"

"In any case," I said, "they seem to experience fear, just like humans. Who knows? To them, we might be objects of horror, nightmares made real..."

"They're afraid, obviously. But they also seem—fortunately—to be tormented by a powerful desire to learn more about us. If only it were so simple to understand us! But look, here comes the night, which will condemn us to incapacity in a mater of minutes!"

He had no sooner pronounced these words than my resolution was made. I went up to him and, placing my hand on his shoulder, explained to him that there was a means of avoiding the sleep. I also explained the reasons for which I had not thought it appropriate to tell him about it. He forgave me—it would have been difficult for him to do otherwise—but I understood, all the same, that he could not help feeling a certain resentment towards me. To ward that off, I continued to justify myself.

"Now that you're...that you're cured, do you see, I've immediately put an end to the necessary concealment."

"Perfectly! I don't hold it against you. Why would I? It's all right. You're a sly one, you know how to dissimulate! My compliments! Ha ha...." He laughed, but the laughter rang slightly false. "I'm cured," he continued, "and I observe with pleasure that it took you some time to recognize the fact. I beg you, though, to avoid giving me the feeling, by paying particular attention to my words and gestures, that you still fear a relapse...that, I couldn't forgive."

"But what makes you think that?"

"You're intent on making me say more than I want to? Fair enough. Well, if perchance you don't know, the malady that I had is called madness, and everyone knows that someone who has been mad might go mad again some day. I don't want you to think that I might do that at any moment. I've been mad, but I'm no longer mad; forget that I ever was."

He repeated several times more, in a threatening and challenging manner: "I'm no longer mad!" Confronted by that ominous excitement, I feared that the frightful dementia might get its claws into him again at any moment.

Ten minutes later, we were lying in ambush behind a bush in the vicinity of the nearest trap-door. Ceintras, who was carrying a bottle of cognac in his pocket, drank a mouthful from time to time, with relish.

We did not have to wait long. Even before the violet light had entirely disappeared, the monsters emerged in considerable numbers. On the threshold, they paused, exchanging hissing noises while shifting their weight from one foot to the other and nodding their heads; then they turned, almost in unison, in the direction of the balloon and waved their short arms agitatedly.

"You know," I said to Ceintras, lowering my voice as far as possible, "I'm convinced that we'll be able to make ourselves understood some day. Setting aside their unexpected and odious appearance, doesn't the sense of what they're thinking and talking about seem perfectly clear to you? The translation is made quite naturally in my mind: 'What's become of the creatures that arrived here by way of the sky? Shall we see what's happening?'—'Are they dangerous?'—'No!'—'Yes!'—'In any case, they're not like the fish in the river or the birds in the bushes; they build machines as we do, and their voices seem to express thoughts.'"

"That's all right," Ceintras put in, shrugging his shoulders. "I entrust the role of interpreter to you—but for the moment, let's try to get closer to them."

We emerged from our hiding place slowly. A monster caught sight of us almost immediately and emitted a cry of alarm. A lively emotion seemed to run through their company. Ceintras and I, determined to see it through, continued to advance, avoiding any excessively sudden movements. We were like children stalking butterflies, creeping towards them on tiptoe, holding their breath. We feared that, at any moment, one of the monsters might give the signal for a hectic stampede. In truth, that would have been very disappointing for us...but, thanks to the prudence with which we effected our approach, everything happened as we desired. A few moments later, we arrived in their midst, the inhabitants of the Pole having been content to continue their conversation in the meantime, while watching us with extraordinary attention.

Then Ceintras—who must have prepared dubious joke some time in advance, bowed in the friendliest fashion possible, and said: "Gentlemen, my hosts, even though you are absolutely repugnant and that we can scarcely bear your company, I'm very honored to meet you."

Their whispers redoubled in volume. For the moment, they did not seem unduly frightened, except that any excessively rapid gestures that we made, unwittingly, from time to time provoked a brief shudder in the little troop lined up in front of us.

"How should we begin?" I asked Ceintras, turning towards him.

"Damn! I think the best thing is to proceed at hazard. Hold on! What if we were to try to get them to follow us to the cabin?"

"I can't quite see how that would get us any further."

"Me neither—except that I recall that our expeditionary habitat appeared to excite their curiosity in the last few days. They'll probably be delighted to receive our invitation? But how do we transmit it to them?"

We tried to use the most naturally intelligible gestures, the signs which, in similar circumstances, are used by men who do not speak the same language. They looked at us, then looked at one another, but did not move. Finally, staking everything, Ceintras—without, moreover, manifesting the slightest repulsion—took one by the arm, as gently as possible, and tried to draw it along.

I watched that maddening scene, my heart beating fast enough to burst. What would happen? With a joyous satisfaction, I saw the monster yield to Ceintras' desire. It released a few squeals, which I interpreted, doubtless childishly, as a prayer addressed to its peers, begging them not to abandon it. The others hopped from one foot to the other again and shook their heads for a few seconds, then broke ranks and followed us, without any apparent hesitation.

When he arrived at the balloon, Ceintras immediately led his companion to the engine emplacement and pointed at it several times. The monster did its best to reproduce these gestures, while turning to the others, who thought it appropriate to imitate it. Evidently, they had misunderstood the meaning of the gesture—but how could we correct their misapprehension?

"They're complete idiots," Ceintras declared, losing his patience. "That's enough for tonight! All this emotion's making me hungry. Should we eat? Oh, that's an idea! We could invite them—what do you think?"

"I think," I said, "that we ought to take that joke seriously. Hunger is a primordial need of every living creature and it's probably worth trying something of the sort."

Leaving Ceintras in front of the cabin, I went to cut a few slices of ham. I presented one of them to the monster that Ceintras had been calling his "new friend" over and over again for several minutes; the creature accepted it apprehensively, studied it, and then held it out to its neighbor; it was passed thus from hand to hand. The last of the monsters, after having examined and felt it like the rest of the band, sniffed it assiduously and put it…into its breast. I saw then that the people of the Pole were familiar with the use of clothing; what I had taken at first for the skin of these creatures was in reality no more than a cloak of white leather that enveloped them almost entirely. On the heads of some of them, it formed a sort of hood. Our precious gift had been stowed away in a pocket!

"They obviously don't realize that it's edible," Ceintras said, laughing.

"Who knows?" I added, "Perhaps they think we might be trying to poison them."

"Let's eat, anyway; they'll understand then that our intentions aren't criminal."

While we ate, they tightened their circle around us. Then, after an animated discussion with its companions, one of them—Ceintras' friend, I think—approached us and offered us two curiously-dried fish that it took from its leather cloak.

"Damn!" exclaimed Ceintras. "It seems that things are going very well; they don't want to lag behind us in politeness!"

"What shall we do with these fish? Shall we eat them? They don't seem very appetizing to me."

"Do as you like. Me, I'll eat mine. I think that's preferable; they'll have no cause to be annoyed!"

I heard the fish crunch between Ceintras' teeth like a crust of stale bread. "Is it good?" I asked.

He swallowed it stoically.

The dawn was beginning to break. The river in front of us had the appearance of an immense luminous sash negligently thrown down on the dark plain. Flocks of pterodactyls took to the air at intervals and passed overhead, little hastily-moving patches between our eyes and the stars. I soon observed that quarrels were developing among the troop of monsters; doubtless their occupations now required a return underground, but some of them wanted to remain in our company regardless. There was a much greater tumult, however, when a new band came to join those that had spent the night with us. The latter were reassuring the newcomers, who were still timid and suspicious, with squeaks, whistling sounds and gestures. Then the quarreling began again; a few blows were even traded.

"Good!" I cried. "They're not so very different from humans as we were able to suppose at first."

"That's true," said Ceintras. "Since they're polite enough not to separate from us without regret, though, what if we accompany them to where they're going? That might cut their dispute short."

"Let's go with them—even following them underground, if they wish. The engine's heavy; they can't have taken it very far. On the other hand, once we've seen it, I don't think they'll dare to contest our right to take it back."

Ceintras, in a decidedly good humor, approved my decision. After furnishing ourselves with a few provisions—and, for reasons of prudence, our revolvers—we went towards one of the groups. The monsters followed us without difficulty, but, as they had guessed and were fearful of our intentions, they huddled together for a few minutes a short distance from the trap-door, and then launched themselves into the tunnel with an extraordinary agility. The metal panel closed again in front of us before we could recover from our surprise. In his disappointment, Ceintras had no other consolation than that of pouring the entire stock of injurious or simply malevolent epithets that he had in is memory upon the heads of the people of the Pole.

During the two nights that followed, there was no progress in our relations with the monsters. We even noticed that, after they came out, they no longer neglected to close the doors, through which we had resolved to enter surreptitiously. Time was pressing, however; scarcely any hydrogen remained within the envelope of the balloon, and the reserves that we had in the canisters were only just sufficient for our return journey. Penetrating into the mysterious subterranean world then became an obsession. We resumed talking, in all seriousness, about blowing up one of the doors, but we renounced that means because it was too violent not to risk irritating our hosts. Opportunity was bound to furnish us with some ingenious stratagem.

At the end of the third night, a troop of about 40 monsters appeared on the river bank and, without taking overmuch notice of us, some of them set about unrolling a large net comprised of thin strands of leather. Soon the troop divided into two groups, which each took one end of the net; then, the one nearer to the river waded into it unhesitatingly and swam across in a marvelously lithe fashion. When the net, drawn tight and maintained under water by weights, had blocked the entire width of the river, the two crews hastened upstream and downstream for some 50 meters; afterwards, those monsters who had already crossed the water swam back to their companions—and the net, full of fish, was eventually hauled back on to the bank.

A little later, while the monsters recommenced their operations elsewhere, we encountered a sort of cart half full of fish in front of one of the trap-doors, which was larger than the others. The door remained inexorably closed, but it seemed certain that it would have to open imminently to let the cart in; its dimensions were rather large. I think the idea of hiding inside it came into Ceintras' mind and mine at the same time.

"Ceintras," I murmured, a trifle pale, without taking my eyes off the cart.

"Yes, yes, I know what you're going to say."

"Well?"

He pointed at the silvery mass of fish, many of which were still alive. "Aren't you a bit disgusted by the thought of burying yourself under that?"

"I'd certainly prefer a litter of velvet and silk, but out hosts have forgotten to put anything of that sort at our disposal."

"A sorry apparatus for the reception of humanity's first ambassadors to the people of the Pole!"

"Obviously, but time's pressing—here's the dawn…and it might be a unique opportunity."

"Oh, a unique opportunity indeed!"

"Do as you like, then—you're a free agent. Me, I'm going to have a go."

Ceintras, as I had expected, gave in. Overcoming our repulsion, we hid between two layers of little cold bodies, moist and viscous, whose crushed spines cracked beneath us and which thrashed about in the final stages of asphyxia on our hands and faces. Already more than half suffocated by their noxious odor, we were convinced that we would choke to death by the time the monsters, as they returned to their subterranean dwellings, piled more fish on top of us to fill the cart completely. We hollowed out a passage as best we could by which the air could reach our mouths; then we felt the vehicle get under way.

An instant later, the repeated echoes of the noise that it made as its wheels rolled told us that the open firmament no longer extended its limitless vault around us, and that we were in the bowels of the Earth, heading into the unknown.

XI. Subterranean Excursions

"Watch out," Ceintras whispered in my ear. "The critical moment has arrived!"

The cart had stopped suddenly, and—I don't know why—I felt certain that we had just left a narrow corridor to enter into a vast hall. In low voices, we held council. Should we wait, or emerge from our hiding-place immediately? Ceintras made an observation that terrified me: the fish that one of the monsters had offered us had been very dry, almost charred...what if they were content, after fishing, without any preliminary preparation, to push the metal carts into the ovens?

"Damn it!" I exclaimed. "That's a risk we shouldn't run!"

Then I realized that, in my emotion, I had spoken too loudly; in any case, it was futile to hesitate any further as to what decision to take. We emerged, dirty, damp and stinking, from our hiding-place. One glance sufficed to assure us that we were alone, for the time being, in the kitchen—or one of the kitchens—of the polar community.

It was a circular room about 30 meters in diameter, the ceiling of which, supported by four granite pillars, formed a sort of cupola. The place was not without a certain majesty. Gutted fish lay on long stone tables; in the middle of the room, between the four pillars, we found a sort of immense grill made of thin parallel strips of iron, which were heated to high temperature by an electric current. I discovered this detail, to my cost, after carelessly resting a hand on the apparatus.

As anticipated, the monsters were not long in putting in an appearance. To Ceintras' considerable chagrin—he had rejoiced in advance about "the expression on their faces when they discovered the trick that we had played on them"—they did not seem unduly amazed. In actuality, it would have been difficult to read the feelings they were experiencing in their faces. We could not even be sure that they were talking about us; the attitudes struck in various circumstances of social life are so often opposed to those that nature and logic seem to indicate! Is it not ill-mannered, in our civilized countries, to point one's finger at the person to whom one is talking?

In any case, they went rapidly to work, without appearing to pay any great attention to us. Some cleaned the fish, others laid them out on the grill; others emptied the carts. The latter contented themselves with looking at us intently when they arrived at the cart in which we had hidden ourselves, and whose cargo we had surely damaged.

The loud gasps of machinery reached us via the four tunnels that ended in the polar kitchen. We decided to follow one of them at random. If, as everything led us to believe, the people of the Pole had stolen our engine in order to study its operation, it must now be in the domain of the technologists and scientists, not that of the cooks. Besides, it was necessary to admit—however insane it might seem—that the primary motive for our subterranean expedition was no longer so clearly-impressed on our minds, and that, for some time, an awestruck curiosity had been the sole inspiration for our research and our ventures.

We therefore went into one of the tunnels, without provoking the slightest resistance on the part of the monsters. They were so busy—or, to put it more accurately, so intimately absorbed in their work—that it seemed to us almost inconceivable that any of them, for any reason, could be distracted for an instant. Moreover, that harmonious intimacy between the workers and their work never ceased to strike us with admiration no matter how long our sojourn in the Pole's subterranean regions continued. The livid beings bearing mysterious objects that we encountered as we walked scarcely turned to glance at us...

Meanwhile, the sound of machinery continued to grow louder; it was as if we were arriving in the very heart of that active, frenetic, prodigiously living world, and that we had been sucked into one of its arteries by the movement of its own life. We finally emerged into a new hall even larger than the first, in which, at brief intervals, an enormous piston of gleaming metal rose up to the ceiling and then disappeared almost entirely, swallowed up by a rectangular well lodged in the floor. Controlled by this drive-shaft, a quantity of machines filled my ears with their multiple hum.

At first sight, there seemed to be no monsters in the room. Having made a tour of it, however, we discovered two of them at the top of a platform set into the wall, almost at ceiling-height. A sort of ladder led up to the platform on which they had just appeared. We gradually grew bolder, and, without even having any need to consult one another, we went to observe them at their post.

When we pass through a human village, the image of each individual is reflected within us, accompanied by various impressions that are translated by specific words such as *old, young, ugly, pretty*...until now, though, we had experienced nothing similar in confrontation with the inhabitants of the Pole. They were all equally horrible, similarly clad in white leather, and almost as difficult to distinguish from one another at first glance as dogs of the same breed in a kennel. Once we arrived on the platform and came face to face with the monsters we found there, however, we had for the first time, in considering one of them, a perfectly clear impression of extreme old age, relative to creatures of that species.

It was bent over an apparatus whose appearance was reminiscent of a typewriter, occasionally placing one or other of its long fingers on the keys that presumably controlled, by means of electricity, the machines whose drone reverberated beneath my feet. It was also looking with sustained attention at a horizontal needle, which was oscillating close by above a graduated plate. When the point of the needle began to approach a line drawn in the middle of the plate, the old monster pressed a lever situated to its left, and the needle gradually moved back. Ceintras, apparently quite reasonably, concluded that it must be a pressure-gauge—but the mechanic's physiognomy interested me more than these mechanical details.

Frightfully wrinkled, the eyes dull and oozing, its body, immediately below the inferior lip, swollen by multiple folds of jaundiced and parchment-like skin, even more hideous—if that were possible—than the majority of its fellows, this individual nevertheless inspired in me a strange respect, by virtue of the age and wisdom I divined within it. On our arrival, without even turning toward the monster of ordinary appearance that stood motionless by its side, it emitted two or three brief hissing sounds, to which the other replied even more briefly. The meaning of that conversation seemed evident to me:

"Are these the singular creatures about which you talk incessantly?"

"Yes, it's them."

After which, without taking 15 seconds to look at us, it went back to moving its hands methodically over the lever and the keyboard.

We departed again at hazard along the first tunnel that offered itself, without knowing where we were going, and without fear of subsequently being unable to make out way back to the balloon an the open sky. Curiosity was literally intoxicating us; we scarcely had time to astonish ourselves with an unexpected spectacle or an object of mysterious purpose, or to get excited about a machine, before we were burning to contemplate something even more unexpected, mysterious or admirable.

I shall not waste time telling you about our explorations in detail and describing the successive sentiments to which they gave rise. I cannot, in all conscience, attach to what I am writing any but a documentary importance; it seems best, at present, to give a general summary of what we saw and to explain the necessarily hasty, and doubtless often mistaken, conclusions that we felt entitled to draw.

What strikes one at first glance in the polar world is its exiguity. The violet light and the heat, and the life and civilization that are its consequences, extend throughout a circular domain whose diameter cannot much exceed a dozen leagues.

The subterranean tunnels radiate within a considerably lesser space. One evidently finds oneself in the presence of a parcel of the Earth that was spared, when the eternal ice-fields of the Pole were formed, for reasons of which one, at least, is not discernible even today—which I shall explain in due course. At any rate, our exploration provides a decisive argument in favor of the thesis according to which the ice of Poles, on Earth and its neighboring planets, were formed abruptly, in the wake of great natural cataclysms.

Thus permanently separated from the rest of the world by insurmountable walls of ice, a few individuals of a species then existing—a kind of iguanodon, or something analogous—were able to continue to live in the immediate vicinity of the North Pole. Given that, one imagines that the immediate necessity of a desperate struggle for existence in conditions so unfavorable must have given an enormous boost to the general progress of the species, and that it developed intelligence in an era when the ancestors of humankind were destined to remain for a long time yet in the limbo of that possibility.

If the region of the Pole has not been condemned, like its surrounding territories, to bear a permanent burden of sterile and mortal ice, it is due to the presence in that place of an immense natural heat-source. It is probable that the waters of the ocean, engulfed in the depths of the Earth not far from the continent where I am located, are heated to boiling-point by contact with the interior fire, and return thereafter through various sorts of channels to the proximity of the surface. They even spurt out here and there in salty geysers, which we would have discovered on the day after our arrival if we had extended out excursion a little further beyond the hills.

What is certain is that the polar monsters have known how to make use of the force seething in the heart of their world for an incalculable number of centuries. Having never had anything to expect from the sky or the Sun—all those natural virtues which humans have been so long accustomed to take for he attributes of God or the consequences of His bounty—they now provide us with marvelous proof that, after having eventually transformed the force at their disposal into the very principle of life, all creatures endowed with intelligence and reason risk falling victim to the illusion of supposing that it is their unique Providence, reserved for them alone.

At the majority of the crossroads of the polar world, one can hear the tumultuous growl of the boiling water imprisoned in enormous metal pipes. Once, having followed a tunnel that sloped steeply downwards for some time, we actually reached the rim of a colossal gulf, full of suffocating vapor, into whose invisible depths the subterranean river, or one of its major tributaries, fell in a cataract and was redirected with a thunderous noise. Within the opaque mist, we could just about make out, a few meters away from us, an immense wheel—the frightful phantom of a machine—which, moved by the force of the waterfall or the current, turned with indescribable velocity.

It is beyond doubt—and it seems to me that I can now present this fact, which a few moments ago might have seemed impossible to imagine—that the polar monsters manufacture their own daylight by using that formidable and inexhaustible source of energy. By what method? Ceintras once believed that he had found the key to the mystery—a secret whose value is incontestable—but he is no longer here at present to repeat a demonstration to which I was only ready at the time to lend a distracted ear and an attention accustomed to finding scientific matters arduous. What I do remember is that he deemed the inhabitants of the Pole to be extraordinary electricians. I think I also recall that he definitely considered the polar daylight to be the result of a luminous heat of an electrical nature, but I dare not affirm that, nor insist upon it further, being almost sure that everything I have written above will only seem to savants to be unintelligence and incoherence themselves.

Having being obliged to remain vague on this cardinal point, it is not without a certain satisfaction that I can now give some precise figures with regard to the duration of the polar day and night. As I had established on the first occasion when it was possible for me not to succumb to the sleep, the duration of the night was rather brief; between the complete disappearance of the violet light and the first signs of its return, I observed that the time varies at ground level between three hours 35 minutes and three hours 44 minutes, and below ground between three hours 24 minutes and three hours 35 minutes.

It was when we spent the night in the room where we had encountered the old monster, and in the rooms situated on the same level, that we observed the minimum duration, from which I think the conclusion can be drawn that the duration increases in proportion to the distance separating the place—above or below it—from the level where we were. The daylight is no different in the subterranean part of the Pole from the surface, and is almost the same in the rooms and tunnels situated below the level in which it is not a question of rising up from the floor but descending from the ceiling. As for the day, it last about six and three-quarter hours.

It is the observation of the stars and the Sun that has furnished humans with the principles on which they base their measurement of time. At the Pole, though, the Sun is a useless object and one pays scarcely more attention to the stars in the sky than to the stones of the plain. To make practical measurements of duration, the people of the Pole make use of clay pots of various sizes, from which thin trickles of water escape. Some such pots are, for example, used to measure the cooking-times of fish, others the duration of the night, and others the duration of the day. One of the last—which are, of course, considerable in size—had been attached to the wall of the platform where the old monster sat.

One day, when we had decided to examine the old monster's work minutely, we took up positions beside it and its young companions until the moment when the water stopped running; immediately bending down, it pushed a lever set between its feet. Then the machines gradually ceased to hum, and, in less than a minute, it was dark: a pitch-black darkness, only punctuated in our vicinity by the monsters' four eyes, shining like carbuncles.

The older of these two creatures was, therefore, one of the most important individuals in the polar community; one mistake, failure of memory or moment of distraction on its part might have resulted in a whole series of disastrous consequences; cold, darkness, the temporary suppression of individual and social activity, scourges that it was equally capable of unleashing in a fit of anger, for reasons of vengeance, or even—this did not seem absurd at the time to my limited and scatter-brained human mind—as a result of whim or caprice.

What great prestige, among the inhabitants of the Pole, in that world where everything—even the elementary conditions of life—was produced mechanically, the individual who watched over the functioning of the cardinal machine must enjoy! It was obviously a king to them, perhaps even a god...such were the thoughts that came into my mind at first—but subsequent observations modified them considerably, or at least proved to me that pronouncing or writing, with respect to creatures so different from us, such words as *respect, prestige, royalty* and *divinity*, involves the necessary influence of a presumptuous anthropomorphism. It is probable—and I am content to say that it is probable—that their intellectual notions do not differ essentially from ours, that the theorems of geometry are true for them as for us, but what is certain is that their mentality and their morality retain none of the confused collections of hereditary habits which those terms serve to represent in human languages.

That world being closed, like a prison, the number of its inhabitants has to be rigorously limited, in the interests of the very survival of the species, and none can live there without having an express reason to live, without performing an exact and inevitable task. Humankind is too vast and too complex not to be separated by centuries, as yet, from the day when it will realize its social ideal, if it is ever to be realized; even in the most optimistic eyes, our mores, laws and present governments cannot be anything but rough sketches, if not ridiculous caricatures, of that inaccessible or infinitely distant ideal. By contrast, in the polar microcosm, everything is so marvelously regulated and ordered that, confronted with the least manifestation of its activity, one has the impression of the harmonious determinism that presides over the movement of machines.

If an organ of that machine is defective, it is suppressed, without vain and wretched pity, and replaced by another that is ready to hand. Indeed, it did not take us long to establish, in the course of our subterranean exploration, that certain monsters—especially those charged with important and difficult functions, whose exercise required a certain skill—always had a "double" by their side: a motionless and attentive companion from which it never separated, and would indubitably be its eventually successor.

We witnessed three such suppressions almost consecutively. They simply cut their own throats, without any of their fellows who witnessed that strange operation appearing to manifest any anxiety. Once again, I emphasize that it is impossible for a man to read sentiments with any certainty on such faces; however, the attitude of the victims, the tranquility with which they presented their throats to a machine from which a kind of dagger emerged, after tripping a switch with their own hands, forces the conclusion that the right to life that humans base so unthinkingly on the faith of a few prophets is replaced among these polar creatures by a profoundly-rooted conviction of the necessity of death in certain circumstances.

Furthermore, old monsters are extremely rare; so far as I am concerned, while I lived among the people of the Pole, I am almost convinced that I only encountered the one. And, to speak frankly, if one excepts a few functions for which great experience and extreme moderation are the requisite qualities, it is quite evident that, beyond a relatively unadvanced age, the individual becomes inferior in himself and in his work. By virtue of an inexplicable aberration, the most important jobs in human society are confided to old men. What might the strength and the vitality be of a nation morally and materially directed by men under 40? What about the respect due to old men? Does respect consist of letting them fill, with fatal inca-pability, various missions that others could carry out much better? But people say: it is their due, and, after all, affairs take their course anyway; let them die at their post; no one will suffer!

Thus gerontocracy hinders human progress. Does than mean that it is logically necessary to dispose of old people, or to set a certain age-limit on life among humans, as at the Pole? No, since humankind possesses a vast and rich domain, which permits it to support useless individuals without immediate detriment. It is sufficient to generalize the system of pensions, to make it obligatory beyond an age varying according to function, and not to accord more importance than it merits to powerlessness. At the Pole, though, given the necessity of realizing maximum energy with minimum encumbrance, it was soon necessary, and probably always will be, not to let anyone die of old age.

Moreover, the suppression of one monster or another is not simply a matter of negative interest, since others take on the job of stripping it down, in order to manufacture grease and leather. This explains why we mistook, at first sight, the white leather clothing that was so perfectly adapted to the monsters' bodies for their own skin. Some of them even con-serve the leather of the cranium and transform it for their per-sonal usage into a bizarre and complex kind of hood. We sub-sequently discovered that this was the distinctive apparel of females. Is feminine coquetry a sentiment so profound and essential that it is able, to the almost absolute exclusion of any other, to coexist in a certain measure in two radically different races?

As for the grease, even though there are mineral deposits of oil at the Pole, and the monsters are not ignorant of the art of its extraction from the ground, they usually make use of it to reduce the friction of the most delicate parts of their ma-chines. Before crying out in horror about all that, remember that the polar fauna does not include any large animals and that, in order to produce grease and leather—indispensable materials—the people of the Pole are forced to made do with the elements that are available to them.

A short time after leaving the hall in which the vast gleaming piston operated, we happened upon a veritable nursery. Under the surveillance of a few females, we saw some 20 little monsters frolicking—who, at our approach, seized by a mad terror, ran to bury themselves in their guardians' laps. They had enormous, disproportionate foreheads, across which clusters of thick throbbing veins radiated above each eye. Their skin was milky white; the appearance of their limbs gave an extraordinary impression of fragility, or even inconsistency, and—despite my curiosity—I dared not pick up the one who passed within range of my hand as it fled, for fear of crushing or breaking it.

All around the room—definitive proof of the saurian nature of the people of the Pole—eggs were lined up in apparatus similar our artificial incubators. Their dimensions were very similar to those of ostrich eggs, but, in the absence of any calcareous tegument, hey only had a blue-tinted translucent membranous envelope, through which the hunched silhouettes of embryonic monsters were visible.

A few days later, we even witnessed the mass hatching of these eggs. The hatchlings, which were almost immediately capable of coming and going by themselves, were examined by ten monsters of both sexes, who carried out an assiduous triage, placing some in little niches built into the walls and carelessly cramming the majority into iron cages. Afterwards, two other monsters arrived, opened a tap set in a corner and filled a metal basin with boiling water, into which the cages and the wriggling creatures were unceremoniously plunged. We were able to witness this spectacle without experiencing any sentiment of revulsion or nausea; that was just as well when, a few moments later, we had the opportunity to see how this atrocious ceremony terminated.

The animation in the nursery became greater and greater. The people of the Pole ran from every direction; the room was soon crammed, and some posted themselves in the doorways to prevent others from coming in and to expel some of the late-comers. When the water from the two polar clocks that were set above the basin had completely run out, the cages in which the young monsters had been boiled were taken out of the water, after which the crowd shared them out equitably and set about eating them, with various gestures that expressed—without any possible doubt—the most vehement satisfaction.

Night fell abruptly from above. By the light of the lantern with which we were equipped, we were able to see the old monster from the platform arrive, who was allowed privileged entry now that his work was done, and who took his part in that repulsive feast with solemn and joyful chewing-noises.

It should be noted in passing that this was the only opportunity we had at the Pole to observe something resembling, nor nearly so, a communal meal. In general, the monsters, at any hour and without interrupting their work, nibbled a few scraps of fish or roasted pterodactyl, of which they always had an ample provision in their pockets.

I realize that no one reading this story will be able to feeling the same horror that I experienced. It must be said, though, that there is not as much legitimate reason for that horror as our human viewpoint imposes. An open or merely sane mind will concede that there is nothing absolute or ideal about the human point of view. For one thing, it is not, strictly speaking, their children that the polar monsters eat; the word "family," as it is understood in our language, is meaningless to them. Reproduction, in their society, is definitely considered as a general mission in which each individual must share in addition to its particular work; there are neither fathers, nor mothers, nor children.

The eggs, immediately after being laid, are handed over to functionaries who hatch them by means of a mechanical process; they are anonymous and belong to the collectivity. On the other hand, do not forget that, for the polar race, it is a matter of life or death that the population should not exceed a certain number; it is therefore necessary to sacrifice some of the little ones. Given that, one can also excuse the people of the Pole for letting those condemned to death be born and then eating them, since they thus procure, by the same token, and without overmuch trouble, nourishment that they consider substantial and succulent.

In any case, to demonstrate that certain rules of morality that are deemed eternal and indefeasible vary according to time and place, even in the very heart of the human fatherland, I recall that 50 years ago, among certain people of Oceania, it was the duty of a respectful and well-brought-up son to cut the throat of his aged father and eat the flesh thus provided...

I have no intention, you understand, of writing a panegyric in praise of polar customs; I limit myself to observing that all these customs are the consequence of a clear-sighted and implacable rationality.

It was over a period approximately equivalent to a terrestrial week that we collected these observations at hazard; they were, of course, completed and gradually organized in my mind afterwards. By that time, thanks of the facility with which the monsters always seemed to give their consent to actions that we accomplished, regardless of their desires, we were able to go into the polar world as we pleased. The trapdoors remained open, in daylight as in darkness. Even though we were equipped with an acetylene lamp and a healthy provision of carbide, we took advantage of nightfall to go and eat or sleep in the balloon. At that time, besides, the underground of the Pole no longer offered any great interest. The hum of the machines had paused, there was no longer anything but silence and immobility in the long tunnels, and, while some of the monsters lay down on the ground to take the few minutes of rest with which their bodies are content, the others wandered along the river bank in search of plants to gather and fish to catch, or hunted pterodactyls in the caves of the hill.

It was entirely by chance that we found ourselves confronted by our engine, when the concern of its recovery had been relegated to second place in my mind, preoccupied with so many marvels. It was lodged at the back of a large recess hollowed in the wall of a tunnel along which we were passing for the first time. Solid bars of iron, embedded in the very rock, arranged vertically in front of it like the bars of a cage, protected it against our potential attempts to carry it off. But whatever emotion we felt at the sight of it was almost entirely eclipsed by that generated by the frightful presence of another object beside it...a human skull!

Yes, slightly tilted back in one of the corners of the covert, a human skull was staring at me with the holes of its orbits. Ceintras, who had seen it at the same time as I had, stood motionless, incapable of pronouncing a word, and pointed at it, with his eyes haggard and his mouth convulsed. When I succeeded in collecting myself, I also observed, in addition to the engine and the skull, various products of human industry that had not belonged to us: a knife, a revolver, a compass, fragments of the envelope of an aerostat and a wicker gondola. We had before us a sort of museum in which the monsters had assembled all the documents they possessed relating to the creatures that, for the second time, had reached them via the aerial route. A name I had heard before reappeared abruptly in the clear regions of my memory.

"Andrée!" I cried. "These are the remains of the Andrée expedition!"

"I know, I know—I've guessed that," Ceintras murmured, as if from the depths of a nightmare. Then his weariness was suddenly displaced by a sinister excitement; he leapt into the air, furiously waving a menacing fist at the void, and howled: "Yes, it's him, and they've killed him! That's the fate reserved for us. Ah, woe betide us!"

For my part, it was a sentiment even more frightful than the fear of death that was tormenting me. I do not believe that Destiny has ever prepared so cruel a disillusionment, with so much refinement, for a thinking creature. I had sacrificed my life to my dream, and that sacrifice was in vain. At least one other man had trod this ground, contemplated this hallucinatory landscape, these horrible and pitiless creatures.

I burst into prolonged and strident laughter, the sound of which frightened me and seemed, as it escaped my lungs involuntarily, to vex, rend and flay the nerves of my throat until they bled. Then I felt my entire being capsize. Leaning against the iron bars that imprisoned my final hope, in order not to fall over, I began sobbing.

XII. False Departure

A few more days went by. Our minds gradually calmed down again, Ceintras' by virtue of his usual versatility, mine when I was able to conceive a reassuring and perfectly plausible hypothesis.

In fact, neither astonishment, stupefaction, nor any analogous sentiment could suffice to explain the attitude of the monsters at the beginning of our sojourn: the unusual precautions they had taken to avoid showing themselves and their hectic flight at our approach. That terror, unjustified by our actions, they almost certainly felt by virtue of some experience prior to our arrival. Doubtless the aeronaut Andrée, gripped by horror, had treated them brutally or cruelly. Perhaps they had avenged themselves in consequence, or perhaps the Andrée expedition had been wiped out by disease or privation. At any rate, at that moment, out hosts seemed somewhat reassured; if our relations remained unaltered—if nothing happened to constrain them—that ought to produce a relaxation of their mistrust.

It was that mistrust that it was necessary to overcome, at any price.

Unfortunately, Ceintras was no help at all. His madness was scarcely manifest any longer, save for stupid or ill-timed actions and ridiculous obsessions, but that was enough to spoil everything. From the moment when we penetrated into the subterranean tunnels, it became obvious that the mysterious force that caused the magnetic sleep was no longer effective upon us, even when we resumed the habit of spending the nights in the balloon's cabin. The monsters had undoubtedly realized that we had a means of avoiding the sleep, but their curiosity had been satisfied and, even if it had not been, they no longer feared to approach us at any time. Ceintras continued, however, despite my pleas, to imbibe large quantities of alcohol.

Until then, we had been able to drink a great deal at nightfall without risk of drunkenness, because the stimulant effect of the beverage was entirely employed in neutralizing the torpor that descended upon us; now, however, when Ceintras talked irrationally or acted inconsiderately, it was more often due to drunkenness than madness. At times when he gave evidence of sanity, he examined the powerful machines with a feverish pleasure, taking notes and drawing plans, and sometimes said to me: "Ah, if ever we get back, what progress will humankind owe to me! The race will be abruptly enriched by all the knowledge painfully accumulated by the people of the Pole in the course of innumerable centuries, like a man out for a stroll who stumbles across an unexpected treasure!"

He always kept these notes and plans on his person. How I regret not having them in my hands now, to append them to these pages. I would certainly have demanded explanations from him had I been able to foresee what would happen!

At other times, our steps brought us back to the engine. For some time—the fact that we had discovered its hiding-place had doubtless been noticed—two or three monsters had been posted in front of it, evidently with the mission of watching our actions. Ceintras was then overtaken by furious fits of anger that I had great difficulty in restraining.

"I don't know why you prevent me from hurling myself upon these stupid creatures," he said, "knocking them down, stamping on them and taking possession of the engine by force!"

Afterwards, he spent long hours grumbling peevishly, cursing the monsters and elbowing them out of his way—and those he assaulted stared at us with their soft and anxious eyes.

"That's not reasonable," I told him, repeatedly. "Calm down, you'll frighten them."

Then he railed at me for what be called my "polar tendency" and claimed that I felt a fraternal affection for those vile individuals. His intervals of good humor were scarcely less redoubtable; he became facetious, teasing the monsters. Nothing delighted him more than blowing the smoke from his cigar into their faces, in order to see them shake their heads in annoyance, and he repeated that joke, which he considered very witty, endlessly. It undoubtedly annoyed them, and they must have been endowed with superhuman patience to tolerate my companion's bizarre behavior as they did.

Meanwhile, as time passed, Ceintras became more and more jumpy—his drinking habit had much to do with that—and I foresaw that a time would come when I would be quite incapable of controlling him. What would happen then? It was impossible for me to be rid of that anxiety for a second.

One day, when we returned tiredly, in silence, to the balloon, a sudden exclamation by my companion made me shiver.

"What is it?" I asked.

"The engine!" he cried. "The engine!"

It took me some time to collect myself. Ceintras' reply had revived a hope which I had not yet dared grant myself; I think I kept my eyes closed for 15 seconds in order that it should not vanish too quickly. But it was necessary to yield to the evidence. Taking advantage of our absence in order not to be interrupted in their work, the monsters had reinstalled the heavy mass of the engine in the appropriate place. Kneeling next to it, Ceintras touched it, caressed it and repeated, in a voice tremulous with emotion: "It's intact…it's intact…"

For the first time since our arrival at the Pole, I no longer saw in his eyes the vagueness and indecision that gave his face such a distressing expression of bewilderment or madness.

"My friend," he continued, "we can leave, return to the company of men. There's no need to wait; I'll check the bolts and test the valves, and this evening, I think that we can say goodbye to the Pole forever."

"First, though," I said, still a trifle anxious, "we have to free the balloon from the magnet that's holding it in place. What are we going to do about that?"

"That's true," he said. "What are we going to do?"

His eyes turned momentarily to the long brown stone to which invisible bonds tethered our machine. "I'll take off the shock-absorbers," he went on, after a moment's reflection.

"I don't advise that," I replied. "Let's wait a while. Since they've brought us back the engine, they must be willing to let us leave, and they must understand that that's impossible while the balloon is stuck to the magnet."

"In that case, why didn't they set us free immediately? Listen, we can't wait for their good will. Time's pressing; we have just enough hydrogen left...and them, what if the change their minds? What if we're misinterpreting their intentions again? Believe me, it's better to get to work without waiting any longer."

We erected a sort of scaffolding made of branches and earth, designed to support the balloon when the forward shock-absorber had been unbolted. The operation was long and difficult, but we carried it through to the end. When we set about removing the shock-absorber, though, it slipped out of our hands and stuck to the brown stone along its entire length. The balloon swayed, the armature beam seemed to fold up...and there was a light crack, followed my a long howl of pain.

I shut my eyes...

When I opened them again, our scaffolding had collapsed as if made of straw, and the extremity of the metal beam was stuck to the magnet in its turn. Ceintras, dragged by the enormous mass as it fell, was lying face-down on the ground, making vain efforts to dislodge his left arm from a heap of debris.

By an extraordinary stroke of luck, despite the violence of the shock, the balloon did not seem to have been damaged. Tilted forward, however, it had the lamentable appearance of having capsized. It was ominously reminiscent of a wreck that had suffered an irremediable disaster. Once more, I felt overwhelmed by the sensation of a power compared with which human intelligence was nothing and against which it could do nothing.

As I went to help Ceintras, something brushed against me lightly. Doubtless attracted by his cries, two monsters had just arrived. They immediately set about talking, waving their excessively short arms in a ridiculous fashion. As if they were able to understand me, I threw myself to my knees in front of them, begging them to help us!

"Vile, filthy beasts!" howled Ceintras, his body taut with pain and anger.

"Try to stay calm and shut up," I implored.

"That's easy to say—but I'm in pain, Oh, it hurts! I've definitely crushed a finger…"

At that moment, the monsters leaned over him. Before I was able for me to prevent his movement, he struck one of them violently in the face with his free hand. The monster leapt back, releasing a cry—then, after some hissing, it disappeared along with its companion.

"My poor friend, what have you done?" I said, to Ceintras, softly. "They didn't mean you any harm; they came to see what had happened, and perhaps to help you get free. Don't struggle like that—you'll hurt yourself even more…"

Crouching down beside him, I forced him to remain still and waited for him to calm down.

Soon, we saw some 30 monsters coming toward us. They were carrying white leather bottles and various strange instruments.

"There's no more doubt now—they intend to kill us!" Ceintras cried, clinging on to me.

"No—look, they're coming to our aid."

The jostling crowd was already circling around us and spreading a thick red liquid, with which the bottles were filled, over the surface of the magnet. The adherence gradually diminished, and Ceintras was soon able to disengage his arm easily. One of his fingernails was almost completely torn away and the whole hand was bruised, but in his joyful surprise he scarcely thought of complaining. Meanwhile, with the aid of metal levers, the monsters lifted the balloon up again. After that, they bolted the shock-absorbers on again, with a marvelous dexterity. Once again, the immense apparatus swayed in response to the slightest pressure.

"Ah!" murmured Ceintras. "They really do want us to leave. They're good, better than humans!" And, throwing himself on a monster that happened to be standing close to him, he took it in his arms and covered it with kisses. The creature did not seem overly appreciative of this amicable demonstration; it extracted itself from my companion's grip and shook itself, while chuckling and looking over its shoulder at him in disgust.

Gradually, all the monsters except for four returned to their subterranean labor. During the hour that our preparations lasted, the ones that kept us company did not take their eyes off us, watching our every movement. We observed that, thanks to the excellent quality of our envelope, it had only lost an insignificant quantity of hydrogen since the inflation that must have taken place at least a month ago. Three of our reserve canisters were sufficient to produce the necessary tension. Finally, the hum of the engine was heard, the gas heated up, the whole machine extended itself and grated...

One minute more and we would no longer be touching that land of horror...

Suddenly, two of the monsters that were present leapt into the uncovered part of the gondola. We thought for a moment that they were going to impede our plans again, and Ceintras was already talking about throwing them out by force— but, attentive to our maneuvers, they crouched down in a corner and remained quite still while the balloon lifted from the ground.

"Are we talking them with us, then?" I asked, utterly nonplussed.

"Yes, if they want to come."

We looked at one another and burst into foolish laughter.

"What shall we do with them, do you think," I continued, after a brief pause, "out there in the world of men?"

"We'll guide them around Paris..."

"Oh! Oh! Can you see them in society, in a fashionable restaurant, on the boulevards, at the Opera?"

"Bah! They'll do very well in a stage-box. They'll be a great success!"

There was more laughter. I was strangely hysterical, and Ceintras, in a fit of good humor, found opportunities everywhere to give loud voice to it. At that moment, though, one of the monsters turned to us, and its expression had something so human in it that I suddenly became serious.

"Ceintras, we're wrong to laugh. Who knows what might result from the contact of their intelligence with our civilization?"

"You aren't about to claim that they're more intelligent than humans?"

"I don't say *more* intelligent, but they're different. In any case, they know things of which we're still ignorant..."

"And they're ignorant of things we've known for a long time. In actuality, there's an unbridgeable abyss between them and us. Then again, just look at them, absorbed since our departure in the stupid contemplation of our engine. They're brutes, simple brutes, I tell you, which will only be of scientific interest to humankind—and when the crowd presses forward to look at them, they'll win us great acclaim in the zoological gardens! "

In truth, my heart sank at the probability of that injustice. Ceintras had certainly summarized, clear-sightedly, the view that humans would take after our imminent return. Not having seen the marvels of the polar world, they would not admit for a long time that these singular creatures were anything but animals...

Meanwhile, despite the contrary wind, we were making progress at quite a rapid speed. The walls of mist that encircled the polar territory were already drawing closer. In a few minutes, the obsession of that fatiguing violet light—which, even when one's eyes were closed, persisted as luminous patches inside the eyelids—would disappear. The two monsters that were accompanying us, leaving behind a universe whose limits were visible and inhabitants countable, would enter another universe of immense extent and an innumerable population.

"Tomorrow, perhaps," said Ceintras, "we'll be asking ourselves whether all this was anything but a frightful nightmare."

"But the two monsters will be here to prove that we weren't dreaming."

There was a silence, which I broke abruptly. "Listen, Ceintras, if you want, our voyage could, indeed, be nothing but a dream. It would all be as if this world never existed. We'll set down, deposit these two creatures, return without them to the world of men and never talk about what we've seen."

"You're mad!"

"No, I'm not mad. But what will become of these creatures in the light of day, in the heat of the Sun, among men who will end up understanding, and will come here *en masse*? You know people as well as I do. You know what companions will follow them to the Pole: cupidity, discord, hatred. They'll destroy the splendid organization and the admirable understanding of this little tribe; they'll disturb everything, upset everything, pillage everything. And if these creatures rebel, and try to resist, men will spread death after ruin, massacring them pitilessly, to the very last one. We can do without them, they can do without us. Believe me, we're acting as conscious accomplices to the most frightful of crimes."

"All that you say is perfectly fair and true," Ceintras replied, "but, given the progress of aerial navigation, others will soon accomplish in their turn the journey that we have been the first to undertake. Since this country must, inevitably, be known to humans soon enough, I'm not inclined to concede the honor of having discovered it to anyone else."

I made no reply. I was forced to recognize that, for the first time, Ceintras had defended his exaggerated love of glory with irresistible rational arguments. Already, only a few 100 meters separated us from the somber grey of the ice-sheet.

His haste to attain what we considered to be salvation increasing as we approached, Ceintras stepped on the accelerator pedal; the panting sound of the engine increased its pace to the point of becoming a sort of jerky whistle. Through the portholes, we saw a crowd of monsters assembled at the limit of the polar world as if to look at us one last time. Then our companions, leaning over the balustrade, both released a piercing cry. We imagined for a moment that they were bidding their brethren a final farewell, but, almost immediately, we perceived a slight shaking; the armature-beam swayed, and it was easy for us to see that we were no longer moving forward.

"They're playing games with us!" exclaimed Ceintras, who was very pale, in a hoarse voice.

"They're playing games with us," I repeated, automatically.

"Ah! But…but this can't happen…they'll pay dearly…"

And, with foam on his lips and his eyes bulging, Ceintras threw himself upon one of the monsters, whose goitrous neck he squeezed in his vice-like fingers. His victim's mouth opened wide; long spasms of agony shook its body—and I never saw such a truly human gleam, as under the effect of pain and fear, in the eyes of one of those creatures…

The other monster had taken refuge behind me, tremulously; suddenly overcome by an instinctive pity, I attempted to implore Ceintras to be merciful.

"See, see! You're supporting them, siding with them against me!" he jeered.

He advanced towards us, threateningly, as if to strike us down in our turn—but the half-strangled monster tried to get up again. Then Ceintras turned towards it, and, being in possession of a large knife that he had found in the cabin, he thrust, cut, slashed savagely…

When the balloon touched down, on a magnet similar to the one that had kept it captive for nearly three weeks, Ceintras was still belaboring a horrid heap of bloody flesh that was still agitated by brief spasms. Rapidly, I helped the second monster—which was almost paralyzed with fright—over the balustrade. While I hurriedly disengaged the propeller, though, and stopped the motor, Ceintras took advantage of the fact that I was otherwise occupied, and leapt down from the gondola in his turn. He hurled himself upon the monster and its fellows, and disappeared after them into a subterranean tunnel that opened nearby.

XIII. The Dying of the Light

I don't think I felt too strong a disillusionment at first. Very often, in my brief periods of sleep, I had had a strange dream that our entire voyage to the Pole was nothing but a dream, from which we would eventually emerge…then came the atrocious awakening, and I had long since grown used to such awakenings. That cruel false departure therefore resembled, at first, one of my familiar dreams, and its continuation into reality; it did not seem to me, in the state of physical and mental exhaustion in which I found myself, to be anything but a continuation of the state of affairs we had been in since our first forced landing in the heart of the polar world.

The landscape was almost identical, except that the region of cold now commenced a few paces away from the balloon. We had come a long way along the river, and from what I could see of it now, narrower and very shallow, it must be very near to its source—which is to say, the ice-sheet. A leprous vegetation of grasses and tree-ferns had difficulty surviving in this region, and patches of ground that were ochreous and bare already showed through, prior to being covered by league upon league of the mantle of ice.

When the polar night fell, the temperature became very low. I shivered for a long time, stupidly sitting in the cabin doorway. But it was, I think, the cold, from which I had not suffered until then, that suddenly made me aware of my new situation and my distress. Then I got up, looked around, and perceived the formless and bloody body of the murdered monster.

And Ceintras? What had become of Ceintras? To what excesses might he have been driven in a matter of hours by his presently-furious insanity? The rapid contemplation of a few images that formed in my mind in the wake of that thought was sufficient to transform my depression into anger. I convinced myself at that moment that Ceintras was responsible for all the things that had gone wrong, and that, if he had not been mad, we would have been able, sooner or later, to make ourselves understood to the monsters.

It was necessary to look at things from their viewpoint: two creatures of an unknown race had appeared among them, which constructed machines, spoke, stood erect, knew the use of clothing and, in logical consequence, must seem to their eyes to be rational—but it happened that one of these two creatures, afflicted by madness did not act rationally. What could they conclude, if not that in our species, reason only existed in a precarious form, imperfectly and incompletely, and that, by reason of that inferiority, allied with an incomprehensible brutality, there was a risk that we might become a menace to them?

Alas, all my attempts to reassure them had been in vain! Ceintras' criminal insanity had just destroyed, in a few seconds, my work of patient wisdom, and there was no need to add to the balance-sheet everything that he might have done since his recent disappearance to realize that the any vestige of hope of setting things in order must now be abandoned.

"Ah," I thought, "my fault lay in believing that the ancient laws of human pity merited observation even outside the human domain. New circumstances dictate new laws and strict reason commanded me to kill Ceintras the minute his madness seemed to me to be incurable. Setting aside all personal considerations, I should have been obliged to kill one man in order not to condemn two to death. In the miserable community that Ceintras and I formed alongside the polar community, it was necessary, profiting from the very example that our hosts set us, to suppress a futile individual who might at any moment become harmful."

After that, as if there had still been time, I went back into the cabin in search of a weapon. In order to pursue his project of frightful vengeance, Ceintras had taken the box of cartridges with his revolver—but mine was still loaded with three bullets.

"Miserable wretch!" I growled, ferociously. "That'll be enough to make sure I don't miss!"

Without further delay, taking up the lantern, I headed for the subterranean tunnel.

A long tunnel extended in front of me without forks or branches, and without enlarging into rooms. I must have covered about three kilometers when I stumbled over a dead monster; two others lay stretched out side by side a few paces further on. From that moment on, advancing with the intention of finding Ceintras, I literally had only to follow a trail of corpses.

The deeper into the heat of the subterranean world I went, the more numerous they became, and the horror of their wounds increased with the number. It was obvious that, proceeding from murder to murder, Ceintras had attained the supreme exaltation of bloodthirsty intoxication. Often, after having slain several monsters with his revolver, he had hacked at them with his blade. Gunshots, almost invariably fired at short range, had blasted away their faces; shreds of flesh hung down like red ribbons from the necks of some victims, stood up in corners into which the murderer had driven them. I shall never forget the eye-ball of one of them, torn from its orbit, hanging at the end of its stalk like an enormous white pearl...

Already unsteadied by the sight of that atrocious butchery, I continued my march with difficulty—in the midst of the darkness, in which my lantern created a feeble lacuna—sometimes slipping on the entrails of an eviscerated monster.

How long did it last? The light suddenly reappeared, and, a short while afterwards, I began to hear a few detonations whose echoes in the corridors and rooms echoed to infinity. For a moment, I hesitated to pursue my course; then I realized what it was: Ceintras, untiringly, continuing the slaughter!

So many dreadful sights had only increased my wrath. Without taking any notice of my fatigue, I went on and on, orientating myself more easily with the aid of the noise of detonations, which resounded closer and closer. The light assisted my progress and the idea that I would be an instrument of justice renewed my courage. Yes, I would kill Ceintras, because it was my duty to kill him; I even promised myself that I would mutilate his corpse, as he had done with those of the monsters, and to persist for a long time, so that the people of the Pole would know what I had done...and it was not a matter of cowardice, a desire to be spared afterwards, that caused me to make that last plan; it was the proud desire to show our hosts that men could, in spite of everything, comport themselves according to the principles of justice.

Thoughts born of fever and sickness, obviously! It is nonetheless true that, at the moment when they presented themselves to me, they seemed to be dictated by the most rigorous logic.

I was possessed by that idea of "necessary reparation" and I experienced a sort of chagrin in observing that the first living monsters I encountered fled at my approach, emitting veritable cries of horror. On the other hand, the sight of them caused me a sincere relief; since I had encountered nothing but corpses for some time, I was almost ready to believe that I would arrive too late, that Ceintras' furious rage might have transformed the subterranean tunnels of the polar world into an immense necropolis.

Suddenly, after a new series of detonations, the light was extinguished. It reappeared momentarily, flickering and uncertain, in scraps of violet clarity floating upon the ceiling of the tunnel along which I was running breathlessly, but went out again a few seconds later.

It seemed to me that I had just witnessed the last convulsion of the dying light, and that the light was now dead. There was only one possible explanation for the abnormal and premature disappearance of the daylight: Ceintras had killed the old monster on the platform, and then its companion—and the machine, deprived of its controlling intelligence, had stopped...

With dolorous admiration, I remember imagining, in a flash, the two monsters—who, seeing death approaching, striking down their ace around them, had nevertheless remained faithful to their task to the end, until death struck them down in their turn, without trying to run away, without even thinking themselves heroic, remaining there solely to conform to the injunctions of an obscure and age-old duty.

I lit my lantern again, and continued to advance. I emerged into a large room. It was the same one in which the old monster and his companion had been stationed, and I recognized, confusedly, the platform, the machines and the gleaming piston, now motionless. A bullet whistled past my ear; I had caught up with Ceintras. At the same time, my exhausted lantern went out...

Waiting for an opportunity to kill the brute with a sure shot, I hid in a corner.

There was no longer anything around me but darkness: darkness replete with an insipid and nauseating odor of blood; darkness haunted by murder and terror. I could have wished for all my senses to be neutralized, and I put my hands over my eyes and nostrils. Then, a seething movement and hectic whispers suddenly informed me that the monsters were coming back in large numbers. What was happening?

Strange as it might seem, I do not believe that they ever had any intention of resisting Ceintras, doubtless because they felt absolutely defenseless against the murderous object that he held in his hand; they presumably did not even perceive very clearly that flight might have saved them. It is probable that the thought that the order of their world had been disturbed seemed more unbearable to them than anything else, and that they were coming, whatever it might cost, to attempt to get the light-manufacturing machine going again. In any case, when I uncovered my eyes, the darkness in front of me was dotted with their pupils. I could not see the monsters; I could not see anything—except for those little patches of greenish phosphorescent light, disseminated here and there in pairs.

Ceintras was moving back and forth, and the sound of his heavy and brutal human footsteps echoed strangely. The revolver shots had become rare; with the pitiless logic of madness, wishing to annihilate a race, he was hoarding his ammunition—but he continued the massacre by means of his knife. From time to time he stopped, and I heard the soft and flaccid sound of his armed fist against the throat of a monster; immediately, looking in the direction of the sound, I saw two of the luminous pupils dispersed in the darkness cloud over and then go out.

And yet, in spite of everything, I did not kill Ceintras! When an opportunity to do so presented itself, a few minutes later, when he passed very close to me, almost brushing against me, I felt the revolver slip from my hands and I no longer had the strength to do anything but weep, while battering my head on the ground...

Hours passed. Had I slept? Had I been rendered unconscious by despair and lassitude? I don't know. Ceintras had left the room; I was conscious of monsters racing away at the first movement I made—perhaps they had thought that I was dead?

I got up unsteadily and went straight ahead, at hazard. Finally, at the end of a tunnel, I saw a square of sky outlined, in which a large star shone...

No, the Royal Magi could not have experienced such a delirious joy at the appearance of the star that informed them of the birth of the child of Bethlehem! I ran, I bounded towards it as if it were salvation. Ah, the softness of the pale and pure air on my eyes and my lips...

I was beside the hill, quite close to our old encampment. It was not long afterwards that I set out to find the balloon again, by following the course of the river.

There are so many resources in the most lamentable of human souls that I soon found myself making plans. I thought of stripping the first magnet of the isolating substance that had restored a brief and illusory to our balloon the day before, and transporting it to the magnet that presently retained it captive. Then, leaving Ceintras behind with neither pity nor remorse, I would attempt to get back to the world of men as best I could...

But I was obliged to renounce that idea; the red liquid had dried out and peeled off, having hardened into thin strips, most of which the wind had detached and dispersed. Moreover, the fragments that I fond seemed to be absolutely insoluble in water, and I could not, in consequence, have used them even if I had possessed a sufficient quantity. My hope was limited thereafter to returning underground in due course and acquiring a few bottles of the precious liquid—but I was too tired and upset to start on that project right away.

I kept my strength up as best I could, drinking a little water and eating the remains of a biscuit that I found at the bottom of one of my pockets. I slept in the bushes, at the foot of the hill, having heaped tree-ferns over me to hide me and escape the potential reprisals of the people of the Pole.

I was as wretched as an animal hunted by men. I remembered a lion that had escaped from a zoo in a provincial town in which I had once stayed, and which had been shot in front of my eyes after attacking several victims. When the exhausted and growling beast saw two men advancing towards it, rifles shouldered, it undoubtedly understood what would happen to it, and shivered, prey to a vague and terrible fear of punishment. To tell the truth, it was my companion who had sewn carnage in the polar city, but there was little chance that anyone would bother to make a distinction between him and me.

I woke up with a start, with a very clear impression that I had just escaped some danger, as if Death had touched me without claiming me. An enormous block of stone was still rolling in front of me, drawn by the momentum it had acquired on the slope. I turned round and saw Ceintras crouched on the summit of the ridge, getting ready to precipitate another boulder in my direction. I leapt forward, aiming my revolver. He adopted a piteous attitude, then laughed bestially.

"Wretch!" I cried, grabbing his wrists to immobilize him.

I fell silent. I understood the futility, at that moment, of speech, the vanity of any reproach. Looking at me with eyes dilated by fright, he murmured something like: "You're making me ill..." Then, when I tightened the vice-like grip of my hands, he asked: "Who are you?"

He no longer recognized me! I talked to him, using all my forces of persuasion, about the balloon, the Pole, our expedition. I pronounced his name and mine several times over...to no avail!

"You've got it wrong," he replied, quite calmly. "I did indeed know Monsieur Ceintras, at one time, but he died a long time ago. Personally, I've been commissioned by England to conquer this land, and I fought a great battle yesterday, victoriously. My weary soldiers are sleeping on the plain..." Then, suddenly suspicious: "Come on, come on...no tricks! Don't get in the way of my plans. Here's a piece of advice: stick to your own concerns. If you don't, I'll have you shot as a spy; I only have to give the order....it's no trouble."

"Ceintras, my poor friend, listen to me...do you remember...?"

"My mission is humanitarian, to civilize. Those people were ignorant of the uses of sunlight; I have just taught it to them. Can you conceive of such a degree of barbarity, eh? *They were ignorant of the uses of sunlight!*"

He rambled on like that for some time. I decided to desist from further contradiction.

After walking for an hour, when we were scarcely a third of the way to our destination, the polar daylight appeared. Ceintras' crimes had not, therefore, been irreparable. The people of the Pole, so cruelly tested, had gone back to work without wasting any time, perhaps having only counted their dead in order to calculate how many empty places to fill...

That was a happy surprise for me: that monstrous daylight, which had previously been a cause of terror and anguish to us, I now looked upon as a liberator—and I must say that, after what had happened, I had scarcely hoped to see it return so soon.

While the ground around us was donning its luminous violet veil again, Ceintras suddenly stopped, assuming the attitude of a man trying to remember something. That phenomenon, which had at length become familiar to us, brought him back to reality. He forgot the glorious calmness of an imaginary conqueror and was seized again by fury. The fury was, at least, not directed against chimeras; it was a considerable but evident amelioration of his mental state.

"Here comes their satanic light again!" he cried. "So I haven't killed them all! Oh, they'll lose nothing by waiting…and then, you know, I advise you not to assume the responsibility of their defense…for I put you and them in the same bag, now."

I seized him by the collar brutally. Concentrating all my will-power in my gaze, I said: "Listen! You recognize me now; you know who I am and who you are; you've no more excuse for being mad. Well, as true as you're Ceintras and I'm de Venasque, and that I have you in my power, trembling and cowardly, if you so much as express the desire to commit new atrocities, I'll kill you—kill you on the spot. There!"

Pale—frightfully pale—his beard ragged, his lower lip slack and moist, his hands and clothes soiled with mud and blood, he stood before me, the most abject and wretched of human beings. For a moment I almost gave in to disgust and pity, but he seemed to sketch out a defensive gesture and, taking my revolver from my pocket, I continued. "Not at word or I'll fire! Good. Give me your revolver, right now—and your knife…quicker than that! That's good; follow me. No, go in front. And don't trip up, if you value your hide."

An entirely animal gleam shone in his eyes. But he obeyed. He went about a meter ahead of me, turning round from time to time to look at me sideways, without stopping. He hollowed out an abyss of silence between us, as unbridgeable as the desert of ice, whose misty glacial breath we could now see rising into the air ahead of us.

The daylight did not last as long as normal this time, and night had already fallen again when we got back to the balloon. I think, in fact, that the violence of the sentiments of mistrust and hatred that possessed me entirely had made me forget fatigue and find the journey short.

During the days that followed, I dared not allow myself a minute's rest. I felt certain that, if my companion found me asleep, it would be the end of me. From that moment on, undoubtedly, I renounced all hope of escaping the Pole. How could I return to the subterranean tunnels in search of the brown liquid? I understood only too well that I would not have the courage to do it, that the hideous night of blood and madness would now populate my mind with images powerful enough to repel me every time I tried to cross the threshold of one of the trap-doors.

From then on, to be massacred sooner or later by the monsters—for I could not imagine that they had any other intention with regard to us—or to be murdered by Ceintras in my sleep—for I was equally sure that I could not resist fatigue forever—was all that I had the right to expect of the future, in the final analysis. More powerful than all my reasoning, though, the instinct of self-preservation obliged me to preserve an existence to which death would have been 100 times more preferable. I wanted to live in spite of myself.

Ceintras no longer unclenched his teeth since I had threatened him, and it was only by the expression on his face and his silence that I understood that the madness had not left him. I sensed him circulating around me like a perpetual menace; he was the beast off which the lion-tamer cannot take his eyes.

An extreme need for sleep renders one furious, just as hunger does. Sometimes, when my vertebrae seemed close to breaking under the weight of weariness accumulated upon them, and the flow of blood, at every pulsation, hammered my temples like the blow of a fist, and my eyelids and soul fluttered dolorously, a single sentence resonated inside me, the obsessive refrain of all my thoughts: "I have to kill him; I have to kill him…"

Then the desire to commit murder made my hands shake, and, as if to remind me that my duty was to satisfy it, an unbearable stench of putrefaction began to rise up from the subterranean passages, in which the people of the Pole, busy with more pressing affairs, had not yet had the time to cremate or bury their dead.

If these pages reach the world of men one day—men who live in the comfortable security of their cities—I do not think they will be able to read them without experiencing a sensation of horror. Do I not have a legitimate defense, though, in this instance? And that need for sleep, that overwhelming need for sleep...! Ah, just try to imagine a similar torture, and I shall accept it without any further digression...

Yes, if I had had a powerful and rapid poison at my disposal, I would definitely have mixed it with the food that I prepared, as I had in the past, and which Ceintras swallowed gluttonously, without suspicion...

Yes, if Ceintras did not die by my hand, it is because it was afraid every time that emotion would make me miss my shot. I can still see myself kneeling beside Ceintras as he slept, several times over, putting the revolver to his head or the knife to his throat...but would I not have gone mad myself, if the bullet had gone astray, or if the blade had not sunk in deeply enough, and he had had the strength to get up, tottering, splashed with the blood from his wound, choking or howling?

Once, I was crouching beside him like that, revolver in hand, and he was snoring like a brute. "Kill him! Kill him!" implored the Demon within. And I replied: "Yes, yes...this time the blow will fall, but wait until night falls...I shall have more courage in the night..."

"Kill him! Kill him right now!" the Demon went on...and I truly believe that I was about to obey and that my finger as already pressing the trigger...

Then Ceintras woke up, abruptly.

He woke up, and a leapt backwards...too late. He had seen what I was doing, and I read in his eyes that he understood my intention. He withdrew to the back of the cabin, and as I went out, wishing that the sky would fall on my head, he murmured confusedly: "Traitor! Coward! Murderer!"

Those were the last human words that I heard.

When I came back, after an hour spent sobbing on the river's edge, I found a stub of paper pinned to the cabin door, on which I deciphered these words:

Goodbye. Since you prefer to ally yourself with the people of the Pole and conspire with them to kill me, I am abandoning you and returning on foot to the world of men. I beg you not to harbor any anxieties on my behalf; I'm big enough to find my way without you.

A sensation of absolute solitude and irremediable abandonment was born in my soul, and overwhelmed it. Ah, what would it have mattered to me then that my companion, if I still had one, had fallen prey to insanity and bee animated by murderous designs? Killed by him, I would at least have closed my eyes upon the image of a human being.

"Ceintras! Ceintras! Ceintras!" I called, desperately.

The daylight faded away. The walls of mist seemed to close around me again—and, abused by a distressing hallucination, I thought I saw a poor voyager beyond those walls, already infinitely distant and minuscule, who was marching, with his lead lowered, striding across the glacial immensity towards inevitable death.

XIV. Written Under the Dictation of Death

How many days have I been alone? Some time after Ce-intras' departure I was afflicted by a terrible illness that caused me to undergo a long crisis of delirium and unconsciousness. How did I sustain my life? How was I able to withstand the lack of care?

I don't know anything, except that I woke up one day, as if from a painful sleep, that I stood up, with great difficulty, on the floor of the cabin on which I was lying, that I went out, very weak, riddled with pains and half-crippled by cold, and that it seemed to me, confronted by the landscape of the Pole, that I had only known human beings and human civilization in a dream or in another life.

"That must be the case," I thought, in all sincerity. "Each of the successive existences to which we are subject is a more-or-less frightful dream, but it is necessary to wake up some day…so when shall I wake up from this dream?"

I don't know anything, except that it must, at present, be winter and the six-month-long night on the ice-sheet. Beyond the walls of fog, instead of the infinite accumulation of vague whiteness that I perceived before, there is nothing but darkness. The phantom of the Sun that remained eternally above the horizon then, never shows itself any longer, and during the hours when the violet light vanishes, the nights are profoundly black beneath a sky smeared with myriads of stars.

I don't know anything…

One sole hope sustained me through my convalescence: that of the probable arrival of other explorers in this world. I recalled that it was in the summer of 1906 that Wellman and his companions intended to take off from Spitzbergen; per-haps, if the resources of their knowledge, their courage and their energy could one day be joined to my present knowledge of the country, it would be possible for us to leave together as we wished, and not come back here again until we had the certainty of being masters of the situation…and I set myself to keep tireless watch on every part of the sky for the appearance of an immense bird of canvas and metal, similar to the one that had earlier brought us to the Pole.

But summer was undoubtedly very far off; if I wanted to live until then, it was vitally necessary to abandon my present encampment and establish myself closer to the center of the polar world, in a place where the temperature was milder. As soon as I was strong enough, I unfastened the cabin and began to drag it, little by little, along with my remaining provisions and a few indispensable objects, towards the little hill at the foot of which I had decided to take up residence.

This labor required a great deal of time and effort—but, puerile as it may seem in the circumstances—once I had brought it to a conclusion and had taken possession of my new domain, I experienced a satisfaction similar to that of a humble laborer who goes to end his days in the country, in a little cottage, the fruit of his savings…

The life of the polar world had resumed its normal course and events soon obliged me no longer to dread reprisals on the part of the monsters. Had they forgotten already, or forgiven, or did they not dare to take revenge? Between these entirely gratuitous hypotheses and many others of the same genre, the last of those mentioned was certainly the least probable. It seems quite likely that the need for vengeance is a special infirmity of the human soul. The animal species considered superior know anger, as we do, but are ignorant of resentment.

While I proceeded with my installation, the monsters did not stop coming to observe me; on the day when it was finished, there was a great palaver outside my door—after which they continued to come and go around me without manifesting any greater mistrust than in the past.

It is during this period of relative tranquility that I have compiled and completed these notes. One day, having extended my stroll along the bank of the river a little further, I came to a place where, after a rather abrupt bend, it reached the cold regions, bearing blocks of ice in its suddenly-accelerated flow, then disappeared under the ice-sheet itself. The sea must undoubtedly be close by, perpetuating itself beneath the eternal ice as far as the Arctic Ocean. Before that, I had only been recording these memoirs to pass the time or to unburden myself somewhat of my oppressive ideas by pouring them on to the paper; after that important discovery, persuaded that there was some hope of transmitting a message to human beings, I pursued my task with greater method and persistence.

I have nothing more to add. I do not believe that I even have the right to hold on to this document any longer, while there is a chance in 1000 that it might one day be found by my fellows, to their profit.

I feel at present that all hope and life are leaving me. My strength diminishes from day to day, and my provisions are almost exhausted. I no longer go abroad; I try, above all, not to think any longer while awaiting the eternal shadow...

But am I able *not to think any longer*? I spend hours motionless, sitting or lying on the slope of the hill and, as happens to dying men, the memories of my past existence present themselves to me with a painful precision. I review the bright horizons, the humble and cheerful cottages on the edge of woods, I think of the towns, the mere mention of whose names evokes the sunlight and the joy of living...children performing round-dances, women smiling on balconies, flowers opening and dispensing perfume...at this moment, in my homeland, the festival of spring must be in full swing...and there are the treasures, the ineffable gifts of destiny, of which I was scornful, which I abandoned in order to go, light-heartedly, to commit the most frightful and complicated of suicides!

Ah, if only I had the courage to hasten my end, to put an end to this torture of regret!

Recently—a lamentable pilgrimage!—I wanted to drag myself back the balloon. It was no longer there. The monsters, understanding that I had abandoned it forever, had dismantled it piece by piece and carried it into their dwellings, as they had done once before after the advent of another. I think that sly curiosity, that need to learn and to take stock privately, in silence, is one of their most pronounced character traits. Have they other intentions? Do they want to profit from our inventions to mount a future expedition to the world of men? I limit myself to reporting the facts, without drawing any conclusion.

In a little while I shall go along the river bank and, as close as possible to the ice-sheet, I shall throw the petrol-can—into which I shall slide this sheet, after the others—into the stream.

May my last words not merely be a farewell, but a cry of fraternity emerging from a repentant heart, addressed to human beings—to human beings who, beyond the walls of my prison, love, work, suffer, live and die as I ought to have done myself—and may God, in respect of whom my prideful folly has been no less futile, guide this message and emit it to arrive in time!

[*At this point, Monsieur de Venasque's manuscript concludes.*]

Epilogue

It was on November 25 last that I finished organizing and copying the sheaf of papers that Louis Valenton had confided to me. It is necessary to say that I had not restricted myself to that task, and that, in pursing my work as an editor, I had devoted myself to an indispensable inquest. I think it as well to repeat here that I would not, for anything in the world, become the accomplice of a hoax, consciously or not, however grandiose it might be—and that, even more so, I would never have allowed the name of my illustrious friend Louis Valenton mixed up in such a business.

Proceeding logically, the first thing was to establish that the heroes of the tragic adventure whose narrative I had just perused were not entirely imaginary. It was sufficient to persuade me to the contrary for me to go to the address mentioned by one of them in Chapter IV. I was received by a dignified and corpulent concierge, who consented to give me all the information I sought, although not without first manifesting a certain reluctance and suspicion. She thought—and you will shortly understand why—that I might be a policeman....

She informed me that Messieurs de Venasque and Ceintras had been her tenants from January to July 1905, that they were very rich men, very respectable, who lived in an orderly manner and paid their bills...that had to be admitted!

"You know, Monsieur," the good woman said, "before going away, they paid me a year's rent in advance, and left me 100 francs for myself in addition." She lowered her voice to add: "Anarchist societies, you see, furnish their members with quantities of gold that would dazzle your eyes!"

"Anarchist societies?" I queried, quite bewildered.

"Yes, indeed! They never told me anything, of course, but I've got good ears...and they were always talking about machines they were building, explosive machines, explosive engines, even! And when their machine was finished, they went straight to Russia, doubtless to blow up the Tsar. What do you expect, Monsieur? Everyone's entitled to his ideas; it's all the same to me, although I don't find that it helps things run smoothly."

I understood. Sufficiently informed, and deeming it unnecessary to tell the concierge, by way of return, that her two tenants' inventions had never posed any danger to anyone but themselves, I took my leave of her, after having allowed her, purely out of politeness to spend a little wile longer lamenting the fate of the poor fellows—who, by now, had surely been captured and hanged, or imprisoned for life in the depths of "Silveria." (I think she must have meant "Siberia," but it did not seem important enough to correct her.)

With regard to Captain Hammersen, there was no hope of obtaining any information, since the *Tjörn*, as I knew already, had gone down with all hands off Cape Haugsen during one of the terrible storms of November 1905, which caused so many shipwrecks on the Norwegian coast. On the other hand, it was easy for me to find Monsieur H. Dupont, the head of the crew employed at Kabarova, who had the other copy of the document and who happened to be my neighbor in Paris.

It was entirely on what he told me that I had henceforth to depend in order to arrive at my definitive judgment. Desirous of getting a clearer idea of the mentality and character of Dupont, in order to be in the best possible position to interrogate him thereafter, I avoided telling him immediately the reason for which I had contacted him, and adopted a pretext. He approved of the stratagem himself when I deemed that I could tell him the truth.

The young man—Dupont had graduated from the Ecole Centrale scarcely two years earlier—possessed, in addition to profound specialist knowledge, a clear and judicious intelligence, and an extraordinary lucidity of mind. He will not take these few lines for flattery, recalling that I only consented to recognize such qualities in him after having subjected him, without his knowing it, to a rigorous examination.

There was no possible doubt. Everything that Jean-Louis de Venasque had recounted regarding the sojourn at Kabarova was perfectly accurate—everything, including the burlesque story of the aeronaut's blessing by the monks. That aeronaut, it should be said in passing, was, in Dupont's opinion, a marvelous technologist, and he was grateful that the profit of Ceintras' invention had not been entirely lost. Dupont had, in fact, received an authorization from Ceintras, on the eve of the embarkation, to make a plan of it, and he was able to show me several photographs of the dirigible taken without the two aeronauts' knowledge.

On the other hand, what he told me about the character of the two completely overturned all my ideas. As will doubtless be the case with the majority of those who read J.-L. de Venasque's story, I had become accustomed to consider him—entirely it must be admitted, on the basis of his own self-judgment—as a rather likeable man; by contrast, Ceintras seemed to me to be an odious creature, and it had been absolutely necessary for me to see him subsequently go mad to find any excuse for him. I learned from Dupont that I was mistaken.

Ceintras was, to be sure, rather cantankerous and apparently not very easy-going, but, provided that the work was going well, he was very pleased with his helpers and even took the trouble to favor them with a few friendly words on occasion. He appeared, indisputably, to have a rather high opinion of himself, but never manifested that vanity and ridiculous love of fame that his companion had not hesitated to attribute to him. And if Dupont had known at that time that one of the two would go mad before long, he would have thought it possible to predict with near certainty that the fate in question was reserved for de Venasque. One day he assembled at his home, in my presence, the majority of the men who had worked under his orders at Kabarova; they were all of the same opinion.

The very appearance of de Venasque did not testify in his favor. In that matter too, the reality did not correspond at all with what I had imagined. I don't quite know why—doubtless because of what he recounted about his childhood and adolescence—but I saw him fairly clearly with the features of a Romantic dreamer astray in our era: a modern Byron, who had launched himself into a heroic and mad adventure out of scorn for banal existence, by virtue of rebellion or *ennui*. Naturally, I had fabricated a noble face for him, worthy, in every sense, of his soul...but on that point too, I was to be disillusioned.

"Imagine," Dupont said to me one day, "legs like broomsticks, a ridiculously narrow chest, yellow-tinted clothes always a size too large, and, planted on the summit of that, a little wrinkled face as jaundiced as its owner's clothes; hair of an indefinable mousy color, parsimoniously disseminated around a pointed skull; narrow eyes, bright and evasive, that never looked you in the face; a nose that resembled a beak; a twisted mouth from which mewling, hissing and strange whistling sounds were incessantly emitted—all of which noises, most of the time, as one could determine with a minimum of habitual attention, were invectives, criticisms, or, at least, observations of complaint at Monsieur Ceintras or myself. There, my dear sir, is the very image of de Venasque. How do you imagine that the people of the Pole, on seeing that, would not have conceived a certain mistrust and apprehension?"

Naturally, as to what happened after the *Tjörn* quit Kabarova to plunge into the mists of the Arctic Ocean, Dupont cannot be any more affirmative than I can. That the balloon had taken off for the Pole, however, could not be in any doubt.

The two aeronauts, who were often in conflict, were admirably united on one point: that of successfully carrying out their audacious enterprise. Ceintras, during the period of trials, only sought reasons for delaying the departure with the evident intention of teasing his companion and paying him back, as well as he could, for the displeasure of being incessantly under his orders. If de Venasque ever took these objections and hesitations seriously, it was because he found them an excellent pretext for accusing Ceintras of pusillanimity.

With regard to the existence of a prodigious and unexpected world scarcely a few 100 leagues distant from the remotest human habitations, Dupont is in complete agreement with my opinion: the account de Venasque had written of his adventures is too rigorously possible to have been entirely invented, especially when one thinks that the narrator only possessed a paltry scientific education; if any inexactitude exists, it is probably not in the descriptions of creatures and things that will be subject to confirmation in due course, but in the explanations that he gives of what he saw and the conclusions that he draws therefrom. It seems obvious to Dupont and myself that, until further evidence is available, it is better, from a strictly logical point of view, to consider the story as true.

A rule that no one dreams of disputing today, after so many surprising and disconcerting discoveries, is that when one finds oneself confronted by things that are possible, however extraordinary they might seem at first, it is better to accept them prudently than to reject them out of hand; this is one of those cases in which the most skeptical run a great risk of being the least clever.

"Science," Monsieur Valenton often says, "has never been more alive and fecund than since it ceased to disdain bold inductions, which, forsaking the domain of the real for that of the possible, sometimes resemble dreams. I never think very highly of a savant who is not also a dreamer; he might accomplish works of compilation or classification that have their utility, but we shall never be indebted to him for the slightest progress."

That view is enough to allow the anticipation that Louis Valenton is as convinced as I am of the existence of the people of the Pole. The skeleton of his anthroposaurus now forms the centerpiece of his collection. We often found occasion to look at it when I came every Sunday, while transcribing de Venasque's manuscript, to bring my illustrious friend up to date with the work done in the previous week. So convinced were we both of the sincerity of what we were reading, we had difficulty at times believing that we were not the victims of a dream—but there the strange animal stood, facing us, set against the window and the sky, as a proof.

When my task was completely done, Monsieur Valenton decided to invite a certain number of scientific and other luminaries to his home. It was a program as sensational as that of a festival that he had to offer them. Thanks to an astonishing coincidence, he could provide his guests with a double dose of evidence that extra-human intelligence and reason had existed on Earth, and still existed today. He put together his guest-list with minute care. He ensured the representation at that memorable session of greatest variety of professions and viewpoints, which could not fail to generate passionate discussions that would be profitable for everyone. In addition, he had exacted absolute discretion from Dupont and me; master of the most marvelous secret that a human being had ever bee privileged to know, until that moment, he expected to experience a rare and refined pleasure in observing the intellectual and moral attitudes that such revelations might provoke in very different personalities, characters and minds.

However limited its animation might be, conversation, even among savants, always unfolds with a certain lack of logic and method. People linger of secondary matters, parentheses opened at hazard taken on an unforeseen importance, the principal fact is sometimes neglected in order to envisage distant horizons...this was what happened at Monsieur Valenton's house. The greater part of the audience, once their initial amazement had been overcome, hastened to admit, in principle, that de Venasque's story was authentic and exact, in order to launch into considerations of what might be done now, of the necessity of a new expedition, of the fate that might, at the final account, have befallen the explorers, of the advantages that humankind might obtain by allying itself with the polar people—or by making use of them, or by annihilating them...

It seems futile to report all that here. What is most relevant to my own purpose is to expose the two principal objections that were raised concerning the authenticity and exactitude of the narrative I had transcribed, in order to discuss them further.

In the first place, someone was surprised by how little time it had taken for the petrol can to come from the Pole to the shore of the Yalmal peninsula. The geographer Girardon took it upon himself, however, to observe that—according to de Venasque's story—the polar river became very rapid at the moment of being engulfed beneath the ice-sheet, and that, on the other side of the ice-cap, in the Arctic Ocean in the same latitude as the Yalmal, explorers like Allard and Müller had established the presence of currents moving from north to south with a velocity of more than six miles and hour.[2] From that, it can be virtually proven that a floating body can easily accomplish the total trajectory in less than four months, and even less than three.

As for the second, much more interesting, objection, it was not presented by its author in an absolutely categorical manner; he had no other pretension than that of opposing to the possibility that we were almost all accepting a different possibility, which seemed to him to be equally acceptable.

Doctor X***—the anonym under which, for the moment, one of our most prominent alienists is retained—did not doubt that the balloon had set off for the Pole; there was nothing astonishing, in his view, in the aeronauts succeeding in reaching it. "But," he also said, "there is, at that point in the story, a fact that struck me because it was within my competence: de Venasque claims that Ceintras was suddenly stricken by madness, when, in the opinion of Monsieur Dupont—who is the only one whose judgment is based on knowledge—it was de Venasque who had all the characteristics of a madman,

---

[2] Unlike most of Derennes' references, this one is probably fictitious; I cannot identify a contemporary polar explorer named Allard, and Baron Ferdinand von Mueller was an Antarctic explorer unlikely to have investigated currents in the Arctic Ocean.

including the physical appearance. Now drunkards, as you know, willingly affirm that it is the crowd around them that is irrational and the ground that vacillates, while they believe themselves to be perfectly healthy in mind and steady on their feet. In the same way, if you introduce yourselves to the presence of two men, one sane and the other insane, and question the insane man, there is every chance that he will tell you that his companion is mad, as you are yourself and as everyone else is, save for himself. How many times, in leaving my patients, I have been able to turn around abruptly in the doorway and catch them shrugging their shoulders or tapping their foreheads expressively with their forefingers—gestures clearly demonstrating that they doubted my sanity!"

According to you, then," a member of the audience put in, "we ought not to see anything in the greater part of the story that we have just heard but the hallucinations of someone mentally ill? The polar people, the violet light, the pterodactyls—all that would only have existed in de Venasque's mind?

"Well, yes," replied Doctor X***, after a moment's thought. "However, it can be that these stories are not imaginary in every respect, and that there is a foundation of reality within them—but the mind of a madman distorts the reality as it reflects it, as a concave or convex mirror does to the objects presented to it. When a sleeper is pricked by a pin, he dreams of dagger-blows...and madness, as one of my masters said, often has the appearance of a dream continued into a waking state."

"What do you think the foundation of reality might amount to?"

"That's something that is very difficult to estimate. Just bear in mind that a madman can construct a world out of very little. Among a thousand equally possible hypotheses, here's one that I suggest to you, without myself attributing more importance to it than it warrants: the balloon, for one reason or another, breaks down within sight of the Pole and has to land. Terrified by the prospect of being isolated, perhaps forever, from the rest of humanity, de Venasque finally falls prey to the madness that has stalked him; then, while Ceintras, attending to the most urgent matter, completes the discovery, he, alone and left to his own devices, writes down what he thinks he sees, with that faulty of imagination and frightful fecundity that one observes so frequently in the mentally ill...

"Consider this: would a sane man, in the situation in which he claims to be, have wasted time in recording his impressions so minutely, and even, in places, with an evident literary refinement, a manifest intention to produce certain effects? Another thing: here is a man who, according to what he has told us about himself, has been prompted to undertake this adventurous expedition solely by virtue of a morbid desire to contemplate something new and prodigious; the first consequence of his madness will be to make him believe that his dream is realized, even beyond his desire."

"But what about Ceintras? How do you explain the attitude that the narrator adopts to him, after his disappearance?"

"Don't you know how skillfully—the skill being due to their fundamental sincerity—madmen recount their lies? Perhaps what de Venasque tells us about Ceintras is entirely his own invention, perhaps Ceintras never disappeared...at least..."

What do you mean?"

"My God, that's an idea, you know...an idea that just came into my mind suddenly...and I wouldn't want you to think that I were intent on increasing the horror of this abominable story by my interpretation..."

"Go on, go on!" The exclamation came from all directions.

"Here it is: think of the passage in which our hero depicts himself holding a loaded revolver to the head of the sleeping Ceintras, and his hesitation over a murder that seems to him to be necessary...imagine that he cordially detests Ceintras, to whose society he has had to submit for months...in brief, what makes you think that he did not kill him?"

At this point Monsieur Valenton spoke: "My dear friend, since, in your hypothesis, nothing is firmly determined, it's obvious that you can put forward anything you please. It's your hypothesis itself that seems to me to be hardly necessary, and very contestable. In my opinion, the story that de Venasque tells us is too coherent throughout to have been conceived by a madman. Permit me also to remind you that de Venasque only had a very feeble knowledge of science...and yet, did you notice the striking exactitude with which he describes, for example, a pterodactyl?"

"There are no beings more logical than madmen," he doctor relied, smiling. "Their associations of ideas often appear bizarre to us only by virtue of the excessive rigor with which they accomplish that mental operation. They are able to go from one idea to another, which seems to us to be separated from it by insurmountable obstacles, by direct and unexpected routes, with disconcerting ingenuity. As for de Venasque's lack of scientific knowledge, I believe you exaggerate it slightly. Did he not admit himself to having seen reconstructions of prehistoric animals in books, at collage? That's enough: in madness, as in dreams, distant memories, inaccessible in normal conditions, sometimes emerge from the shadows with marvelous clarity...

"For instance, I'll give you an example of a subject that I studied recently, a certain Léon Rogue. Perhaps you recognize the individual's name, since he had a certain reputation as a poet while still young. It was two years ago that the unfortunate fellow fell prey to delusions of grandeur. He claimed to be a reincarnation of Victor Hugo and became irritated when anyone did not call him by that name; he wanted to present himself to the Academy and, once elected, to expel all his colleagues, he alone, he said being adequate to the glory of that institution. In a certain stratum of poetic society, as you now, people are somewhat accustomed to thoughts, and even speeches, reflecting such overweening vanity, so no one took much notice at first. It was only after he had ordered several kilometers of black cloth from a textile-manufacturer, with which to drape the Arc de Triomphe on the occasion of his own burial, that his family took the decision to confide him to me...

"At present, he has completely given up all thought of poetic glory; he affirms that he is still an explorer in the exercise of his profession. He believes that he can escape at will from 'the prison to which his enemies have consigned him' and circulate throughout the world *in a manner analogous to that in which words are carried by telegraphic cables*. He even wants to patent this new means of locomotion. Every week, I receive a tale of his voyages. Here's a fellow who has scarcely studied geography since the age of 15, preoccupied as he was in filling the magazines with his produce, recommending himself to critics and, more recently, pleading for awards, with threats to the administrators of never writing another line if they rejected him...well, he nevertheless deploys, relative to the aspect, the inhabitants and the mores of countries whose very names would mean nothing to you, knowledge that would render a specialist jealous!

"It only remains for me to excuse myself for having spoken at such length. The facts that I have told you have, at least, the advantage of appearing significant enough to me to dispose me to an eloquent conclusion, to which you also ought to pay attention."

There is obviously nothing to say to all that, except that de Venasque's madness can only be considered, at the present time, as a secondary possibility, to which an immediate possibility is logically preferable.

I have limited myself until now to transcribing the results of my inquiry and the essential points of an instructive conversation. I hope the reader will now permit me to summarize my personal impressions.

It is not only because logic commands me that I am convinced of the existence of the people of the Pole; I also believe in them for more obscure reasons, by intuition, perhaps even—to borrow a phrase from Michelet [3]—*by virtue of the odor of truth that the story gives off and which, if we know how to perceive it, convinces us better than any proof.* In any case, the memory of what I have read still haunts me pitilessly, and the images are as clear in my mind as if I had seen the objects they represent with my own eyes. No night goes by without my recognizing in a dream an immense violet plain peopled with hideous creatures with goitrous throats and lizard-like lips. Sometimes, in broad daylight, I find myself shuddering violently if someone or something brushes against me unexpectedly—and it is, veritably, as if the world in which I live has suddenly lost a little of its age-old security.

Yes, despite the glacial zone that separates us from the people of the Pole, the idea that we are no longer *alone*, that we are no longer entirely *at home* on the Earth generates a confused and unbearable disturbance in me. It even seems to me that de Venasque did not insist sufficiently on the possibility of an incursion of monsters into the domain of men. Perhaps they now imagine the land beyond the ice-sheet as a sort of Eldorado; perhaps they are, for the first time, experiencing vague covetous desires, and, in consequence, a private disgust for their laborious life. Their natural curiosity will, moreover, largely suffice to motivate their departure in our direction, and if, as there is every reason to believe, they now understand the principles of the explosive motor and aerial navigation, they will set out as soon as they see fit.

I know full well that they are not very numerous, in proportion to the human population of the Earth; I know also full well that they comported themselves with regard to our explorers as timid and inoffensive creatures. If, however, some

---

[3] This reference to the historian Jules Michelet, as the substance of the quote emphasizes, is intended to reinforce the second layer of implicit unreliability that Derennes is now adding to his narrative; Michelet was renowned as a politically committed historian, who cared more about the moral implications of the "facts" he recorded than their mere accuracy.

among them emigrate to places in which there is no longer any need to destroy the greater number of their progeny, they will not be long delayed in multiplying vastly, by reason of their frightful reptilian fecundity.

Furthermore, we might easily be under an illusion as to the cause of their timidity; it is not due to their physical weakness, which can only be apparent, since some of the work they do surely requires a considerable deployment of strength, resistance to fatigue and even to sleep; it comes, instead, from their absolute inexperience of violence and of any violent gesture. Their timidity was that of stupefaction; they did not understand, at first, that furious human desire to kill...but they must have reflected since. What fatal imprudence Ceintras displayed! It is humankind that has taught them murder! And who knows whether, at this moment, empowered by that information, animated by desires for conquest and anticipating a possible war, they are not preparing weapons in their subterranean dwellings against which we will not know how to defend ourselves right away, and whose ingenuity and power will equal those of their machines and their magnets?

I do not presume to claim that things are developing in this fashion, only that humans should understand that it is henceforth necessary for them to be alert and forearmed.

But there are more important things to do. We must, for the sake of human pride, take the offensive. We cannot, for the sake of our race's sovereign past, accept that a part of the Earth, however small, remains unsubmissive to its domination. It is evidently impossible for the polar saurians to usurp the empire of a world whose conquest we have pursued for thousands and thousands of years: a world in which we can no longer take a step without treading on the bones or ashes of our dead, on soil whose every part is mixed with human dust. If, however, they cause us the slightest damage, we must not suffer it—and it is enough to provoke our vengeance and their enslavement that they have caused two of our peers to perish, by virtue of their stubborn, sly and incomprehensible desire to keep them captive in their country.

In any case, that enslavement is not in any doubt, even in the near future. The story of these adventures, divulged to the wider public, cannot fail to provoke sentiments similar to those that I am expressing. We possess, thanks to Dupont's precautions, plans for an excellent dirigible balloon, and tomorrow, airplanes will finally be plying the highways of the sky. We know, moreover, what ambushes must lie in wait for us on the part of these monsters, and it is therefore easy for us to avoid them.

A new expedition is vital. All the nations must participate in it, all of them forgetting their discords for the first time, uniting their aspirations and their efforts against the rival race, and an aerial fleet mounted by them must go to plant on the land of the Pole, not the flag of such or such a nation, but that of the Human Empire itself.

THE END

THE CONQUERORS OF IDOLS

To Franz Toussaint

I dedicate the story of Jean Aruégoyen to you, Franz, because, like me, you love Saint-Jean-de-Luz, and because you almost certainly perceived, noticed and perhaps even knew the hero of this story, during the peaceful season when you used to stroll with Gina Laura along the headland of Socoa. Ten years ago, Jean Aruégoyen, was still eking out his old age there, after an adventurous and wonderful life—which, alas, he had not time to recount to me in its entirety.

Since then, Gina Laura has died, very young and beautiful, at least in the charming book that bears your signature and has her name as its title—a name suggestive of the spring forest and its woven crowns, the golden genista and the black laurel. And Jean Aruégoyen has passed on too, at a ripe old age, to be happy or to suffer in a world other than this, and to see—to employ an admirable expression of the peasants of the Basque country—what life is like on the other side of life.

Jean Aruégoyen was already so very old when I knew him that his death, of which I learned a few months ago by chance, seemed to me to be merely the crowning achievement and supreme realization of his personality. One can remember him and his stories with admiration, and without regret. Follow me in your imagination, Franz, back to Socoa. Let us pass through Ciboure, with its scent of brine and fried tomatoes, and take the coast road, where the eyes are teased by the green and violet light, the nostrils with the spice of mint and the seawind. You remember the inn, don't you? It's vulgar and smoky, with shabby spindle-trees in pots lined up on the terrace—but it's cool there and the cider is good. Imagine yourself sitting on the bench, next to that old man smoking his pipe...he'll gladly accept all the cider you care to offer him.

Then, without your having to ask him, he'll tell you the most astonishing stories.

You have only to listen, friend! I am transcribing—and translating, when necessary—but he is the one who is talking.

C.D.

I

I, Jean Aruégoyen, a poor old fellow in a threadbare beret and a woolen cardigan with holes in the elbows, who lives
on crab soup and cheap wine on a pension of 300 francs, in
whom no one in the world any longer takes an interest—I,
Jean Aruégoyen, who is talking to you now, was once a king.

I was not a king to be laughed at, on carnival day or in an
hour of folly, but a king worthy of the name, the ruler of a
territory a quarter the size of France, populated by nearly a
million well-armed and valiant men who would lie down in
the dust at my word. A proud country, rich in livestock, with
palaces whose like have never been seen in Europe: palaces
that rose up very high in the sky and were sunk very deep into
the Earth, And in these palaces, Holy Mother of God, were
treasures of gold and precious stones such that, even today, I
only have to think about them to feel flames dancing in my
head and vertigo gripping my heart.

Up there on the hill, in that hovel you can see up there,
I'll end my days. When you've spent 50 years at sea, you see,
you can't live without seeing it and sniffing it, even if the
memories you retain of it aren't all excellent! I'm not a man of
the coast, though. I was born inland, at Ustarritz. My parents
were laborers, and I grew up to be a laborer too, until I fell
prey to an illness well-known to our race, which is the tedium
of seeing the same thing every day. It grips your arms, legs
and heart at the same time, and develops into an inexplicable
disgust for everything you've loved, and with which you've
been content until then.

The handle of the plough seems terrible heavy in the suf-
ferer's hands; there's no more joy in sowing the grain or eating the bread; the blue beautiful mountains of our homeland,
as soft to the gaze as silk curtains, suddenly seem to him to be
the walls of an odious and menacing prison. He no longer goes
to the Sunday dances, or pelota games, or those beautiful
miracle plays that were still performed in so many towns in

my childhood, in which God and the Devil argued in our own language, both so handsome in their tall hats, one circled with a crown of gilded paper, the other surmounted by cardboard horns.

Love itself is impotent against that illness, and if the one who is touched by it has already chosen a bride among the slender and pretty daughters of our homeland, she can no longer do anything but weep—poor darling!—for the fickle fellow will break it off the day after tomorrow, no longer desirous of her kisses and smiles; he sometimes forgets that he ever swore to love her forever. And he becomes inert, taciturn, indifferent to people and things alike, his forehead perpetually furrowed by dark wrinkles. Except that, when the wind blows from the direction of the coast—when he hears, even in the distance in the valley of the Nive, the sirens of ships setting off from Boucau, and when the tranquil air of the forests and fields is brusquely impregnated with saline freshness—our young fellow mistakes the wind for the face of a friend, and shivers like a colt inexpertly tethered to a post, deprived of space to roam.

What calls him thus towards the Ocean, towards the Americas, towards the Caribbean islands? No one knows. In my childhood, old folk still said that there was once a beautiful continent between our coasts and those of Brazil, populated by men of our race, and that the ancient inhabitants of America were our brothers. When the beautiful continent was engulfed by the waves, we remained stuck in this corner of Europe, like desperate sailors to a wrecked ship. Perhaps the need for exile that is endemic among our kind is merely the desire, still alive in our blood, once more to see the country that might have been our true and vast fatherland, if we had come into the world a little more than 30 centuries ago.

In any case, when a young man suffers from the illness from which I suffered, it's not merely a desire to go abroad—like some Basques you know and could name—to make a fortune and then come back, loaded with gold, to die in his native village as a man of property; it's also an implacable desire to experience adventures, to wander from one continent to another as you might jump a stream, there to search for something impossible—something like the traces of the beautiful continent drowned beneath the sea. If he amasses a little money in the course of his travels, so much the better—but that's not essential. Most come back home as poor as Job on his dung-heap, enchanted just the same by their sojourn in the underworld—and you can be sure that if he could start his life all over again, he would not choose one different from the one he chose and led the first time round.

Look me in full in the face: me, Jean Aruégoyen, native of Ustarritz, who is talking to you—I am one of those.

My parents were tenants of the Hiriburres, rich and good people who built a lovely white house on a hill overlooking the river, with a perron, and balconies with red-painted wooden balustrades, on which peacocks perched and within which dogs slept. There was a son in the lovely white and red house, a son of my own age, named Georges—and in spite of the difference in our status, I've never known a better or more sincere friend than him. He was only happy in my company, and I languished too when I was deprived of his. His benevolent father and honorable mother, who took an interest in my little person, looked kindly upon that friendship; people in the country are not proud, because, rich or poor, we are of sufficiently ancient blood to consider ourselves as all noble, compared with the Spaniards who stink in the body and the Gascons who stink in the soul—which does not apply to you, honored sir, for such insults have not been justified for many, many years.

In the same way that I had permission to play with Georges' fine toys as a child, I subsequently profited from the lessons that old professorial savants came from Bayonne to give him...until the day when my elder brother went away on military service and I had to bid farewell to books and go to work in the fields, not without regret.

I was not yet 17 when I became sick of looking at the same things, so violently that I was visibly perishing of it. When my poor father understood what was happening, he was the first to tell me to do as I wished, for he knew well enough that the most valiant of lads is powerless against the call of other times and other worlds. They would try to do without me, to work harder, and to address a few more prayers to the Lord.

I remember, as if it were yesterday, my last visit to the Hiriburres. I can still see myself, childishly proud, in my new jacket and beret. When the moment came to say goodbye, Georges suddenly dissolved in tears—less, as I immediately understood, by virtue of regret at losing his favorite companion, as at the idea of not being able to come with me, attached as he was to his home by his wealth...

A full ten years went by, during which I lived as I could, sometimes a seaman on the ships and sometimes a worker in the ports, sometimes succeeding in establishing myself for a few months in a city that I liked and earning my crust by means of a little trading or meager employments. Ten whole years, I tell you! And you'll understand that, even if I intended to relate in detail everything that happened to me I that era, the days that remain to me on this Earth would be insufficient to the task.

Now, when I was forced by a series of bad luck and a few unfortunate occurrences, to sell a little inn—a bar, as they say nowadays—that I had opened a year earlier in the vicinity of Buenos Aires, there was nothing left to do but to take my leave: to pack my bags and set off again, at hazard, to wherever my luck, good or bad, might care to take me.

A ship bound for Chile was taking on emigrants at the time, and I jumped aboard with the few piastres that represented my entire fortune. You've never made use of ships carrying emigrants when relocating? So much the better for you, honored sir, for voyages in those conditions are no pleasure-trips, you can take my word for that. Imagine being piled up in the bottom of a hold, stifling in the fetid atmosphere of the

163

dregs of humanity, smoke and burned oil, living on straw in-fested with cockroaches, lice and those little brown South American rats that cry in the night, in voices almost as sharp, if you'll forgive the expression, as their teeth. Add to all that, after a few hours, the dull noise of the engine, which ends up having the same effect on you as the hammer of an invisible torturer, turning around you, falling methodically and relent-lessly upon your forehead or the back of your neck. Believe me, though, it wasn't the first time that I'd been reduced to traveling like that!

Caught up in that petty unpleasantness, I killed time as best I could by thinking about a brighter and more comfortable future. And when I had finished ruminations of that sort, and drunk a little bitter wine that someone extracted from a can-teen put at our disposal, I began amusing myself by singing songs from our homeland: the oldest ones, preferably those that sounded a bit silly. Well, take it from someone who knows, they're the ones that protect you best against the cock-roaches,[4] whether they're wandering around your body or building nests in your brain.

Now, it happened that one day, as I was exercising my voice on the final chorus of one of those songs before starting on another, one of my traveling companions—as dirty and as pitiful as I must have been—sat up in the straw beside me where he had been snoring and looked at me...and continued looking at me...

"So where are you from?" he said.

"If you can't guess from my speech, you can ask till you're blue in the face...because, if you understand my lan-guage, why do you need to ask me where I'm from?"

---

[4] The word the narrator employs here, *cafards*, has several meanings in addition to its trivial reference to cockroaches, one of which is to a kind of madness that overtakes people far from home, who are lost or desperate.

The man took me by the hand, laughing, and aid to me in Basque: "Good day to you then, my dearest Jean Aruégoyen. Is it really possible that you don't recognize me?"

Then I started weeping like a little child, for the person who had just addressed me in that manner was—ah, now I recognized him as easily as if I had left him the day before!— Georges, my friend Georges, the son of my old masters, the richest people in Ustarritz and its surroundings: Georges Hiriburre, reduced to traveling in the hold like a lost soul, like a pauper...like me!

In my case, though, it was hardly for my pleasure, even less because I had wanted it, that I was living as the most wretched vagabond in the whole wide word, while for him...

I remembered his tears on the day we said goodbye, and I imagined for a moment that my example had turned his head. In reality, the story, although quite simple, was a little more complicated than that. His parents had been completely ruined by the flight of a dishonest banker; they had died of grief—the benevolent gentleman and the worthy lady!—a few months after one another...that was all. And Georges was now wandering the face of the Earth, like so many others of our race, still mourning his parents but personally afflicted by a poverty that had, for him, the miraculous value of setting him free to do as he wished.

We swore to one another that we would never part again, that we would unite our efforts to work hard and amass a fortune with which, one day—which never came—we would buy back the beautiful white and red house on he hill overlooking the Nive.

The pleasure of our unexpected encounter cut the remainder of the voyage astonishingly short. Ah, it was wonderful, I swear to you, no longer being alone to drink the bitter wine from the canteen or sing the old, slightly silly songs of our homeland! Encouraged, restored, full of confidence, we disembarked at Valparaiso as if on to conquered land!

II

Months passed. Occupied by turns in unloading goods in the port, selling maize pap and other greasy delicacies in the low quarters of Santiago, serving as snake-hunters or mining prospectors in the Cordillera, or as fillers and rinsers of thermal baths at Lhai-Lhai, we retired, alas, from these various professions with no other profit than the science of tightening our belts as required and the habit of putting on a brave face when our stomachs complained of ill-treatment.

In a life like the one we had chosen there are, after all, no talents or qualities beneath contempt, and we sometimes contrived to be proud of ourselves on that account—but there's no pleasure in being endlessly weary. Hunger, having prowled around our neighborhood, narrowed its circles around us like an evil witch; at certain troubled moments, I seemed to come face to face with it. In fact, yes, I have seen its face: it's as ugly as Death and just as thinly larded, and it has the same sneering laugh, but it chatters like a loquacious lunatic who has nothing to give you but bad advice, wrath and rage.

Georges, his strength exhausted, finally decided to talk to me: "No more of this, friend!"

That was my opinion too, but what options did we have? Theft? Murder? When hunger whispers in your ear, I tell you, you finish up letting yourself be convinced that it has come to that. There was another solution, which consisted of killing ourselves…and there was, finally, a means of getting out of the business that was simpler but not as radical, but which appeared to us—to Georges as well as to me—to be no less dishonorable.

"What if you went to the consul?" I stammered, lowering my head.

And Georges, in despair, went to find the French consul in Santiago.

He discovered an old acquaintance, Palois in origin, who welcomed him with open arms, advanced him enough to get some decent clothes, and even invited us to dine with him. I remember that dinner: there was a sucking-pig stuffed with sweet-potatoes, and iguana—a fat lizard that one cooks like lobster and which has a similar taste...oh, it was good, good...so good that we kissed the consul's hands, Georges and I, when he invited us very warmly to fill our plates again.

A fine man, that consul! "Let's see," he said to us, "you have no desire, as I understand it, to return to France right away?"

We replied, with touching unanimity: "Oh no—not yet..."

"Well," the consul went on, "I'll try to find a nice little niche for you...and I shouldn't have too much trouble settling the matter in the near future..."

Things didn't drag on, in fact. A week later, slightly flabbergasted but full of gratitude for the consul and no less admiration for ourselves, we were officially notified that Georges had been named head, and me his deputy, of the Chilean Bureau of Indigenous Complaints.

In that era, this was not such a colossal favor as you might suppose. Relations with the Indians of the distant provinces were still rather delicate. As the authentic Chileans did not care to stick their noses into it, the government preferred to employ strangers—people of our sort, pilgrims of the world—who, when the patience of the Redskins gave way to rancor, could easily go elsewhere to protect themselves from reprisals that were often elaborate.

We were dutifully warned about all that, but we were also assured that, unless we committed gaffe after gaffe, we should be good for two full years of tranquility; new faces, in fact, always inspired confidence in the natives, persuaded that the white lords had finally replaced the careless and incapable functionaries with others who would turn out be full of good will, conscience and intelligence. Two years! We had not expected as much as that...

We were well-housed, always at the expense of the State, adequately paid, and our work was genuinely quite interesting.

It consisted of putting on a show of listening to the jeremiads of the Indian chiefs who came from time to time to protest against their peers, their neighbors or the encroachments of certain unscrupulous white men on territories that the white lords themselves had recognized. I say "putting on a show of listening" because we had received formal instructions from above never to transmit these complaints to the competent authorities—an order that was all the more easy to carry out because the competent authorities did not exist. On the other hand, though, we were advised—in our own interests, so that the spell would not be broken too soon—to be prodigal with our fine words and wonderful promises.

So, about a ten times a month, we saw some feathered Redskin chief arrive, draped in his ceremonial cloak, as handsome as a god or as ugly as a monkey, depending on his tribe and race, who, after a quantity of polite greetings and the offer of a few meager gifts, would recite the sorry tale of the injuries to which he had been subjected, against all justice, strongly reinforced with grimaces and raucous exclamations.

Meanwhile, our interpreter, while imitating the plaintive tone of voice and gestures, lit cigarettes and chatted to us about the weather, and Georges—who, being a handsome lad, was a great success with the Chilean ladies—made good use of the time by scribbling a few *billets doux*, confirming in writing the time of some lovers' meeting promised beneath the trees of the Grand Jardin or the Arcades of the Place Santa-Maria. When the ceremony seemed to have gone on long enough, he showed the Indian chief the *billet doux* that he had just written, accompanied by a knowing look, and a little office-boy as mischievous and sly as a baboon would immediately carry it off to its destination—and the interpreter, not without drawing the complainant's attention to the haste with which the white lord was attending to the settlement of the affair, had no more to do than invite the client to go back to his mountain to give the good news to his people immediately.

After that, the gentleman withdrew, not without showering us with thanks, bowing and genuflecting, proclaiming that we were more glorious than the rising Sun and more perceptive than the eye of the condor. We were sure to see him a few weeks later, slightly surprised by the delay, but still dazed with gratitude and nourished on the good bread of trust, and then to see him several times more thereafter. We knew full well that the day would come when the bread of trust would begin to seem bitter to him, and that the situation would gradually become unhealthy for us, but we had two years in front of us, didn't we? And, at the end of the day, we hadn't left our homeland to end our lives sitting peacefully in some Chilean deck-chair…no, we remained there as if in ambush, waiting for a favorable opportunity to go seek our fortune elsewhere.

III

We waited for that opportunity for almost two years, but we had been able to maneuver skillfully enough for our clients not to have found the bread of trust bitter as yet.

One day, I noticed that Georges, instead of listening to the aforesaid clients distractedly, seemed to be encouraging them to talk. The first time I asked him a few questions about it, being rather intrigued, he was content to smile and place an enigmatic finger on his lips. A few days later, when I asked him for an explanation again, he told me that I was quite right, that he was bringing an ambitious plan to maturity, and that "there must certainly be something to attempt in that direction…"

"In what direction?" I asked him.

"That's not important for the moment. Not that I don't trust the only friend I have in the world…but what good will it do to fill you with beautiful illusions, if nothing comes of it?"

"I could help you, advise you…"

"There's no rush; it's for me to advise you of the new situation and for you to follow my advice…you might make a start, though, by learning our clients' language. You can already jabber a few words of it, but that's not sufficient. Work on it! All I can tell you is that we'll get our hands on a fortune if everything goes as I dare to hope."

I noticed on the following day that he was already capable of holding long conversations with the chiefs that came to visit us, without any difficulty.

More days went by.

One morning, as we were calmly sipping our aperitifs in an upmarket café in the Arcades, I began making jokes about Georges' success with beautiful ladies; at that hour, as was their habit, they were going from shop to shop in their national costume, chatting to one another and competing in heaping up purchases in the carts pulled by their servants: the hats, ribbons, mantillas and scarves that would make them more beautiful that evening...

"They're genteel and courteous," Georges replied to my teasing, not without a hint of regret, "with the brains of parakeets, but...but it's as pleasant to caress those little creatures as pretty cats. Just let me have one more good look, my old friend..."

"Do you intend to become a monk? You're talking about them as if you were saying goodbye to them forever."

"I shall—or rather, we shall—indeed be saying goodbye to them forever," Georges replied, sadly.

I understood: the time seemed to have come to attempt the great adventure that he had mentioned vaguely.

"Whether we succeed or not," he continued, "we won't be able to hang around too long in these parts afterwards. Yes, another week, and we'll set out for the land of the Agzcé-aziguls."

"The Agz...?"

"...céaziguls. Open your ears and hold on to that name. If any of our savage chiefs pronounces it in the next few days in your presence, try not to miss a single word of what he's saying. There might, perhaps—can one ever be sure?—be useful information still to be gleaned."

After that, he gave me all the explanations for which I had been waiting, without showing it, with a perfectly legitimate impatience.

The Agzcéaziguls were an old indigenous tribe, whose lands extended over a mountainous desert that was considered almost inaccessible, far to the north in the confines of Bolivia. They were said to be descended from the ancient Incas and, in consequence, from the Sun, in the most direct line possible. They possessed illustrious traditions and fabulous treasures; the missionaries had never dared attempt their conversion, or had not succeeded in reaching them, with the result that they still worshipped their own gods—mysterious and probably bloodthirsty gods—in subterranean temples gleaming with gold and precious stones. Constrained, however, by the ungenerous nature of the place, where they had had to live almost exclusively on their herds, grazed in the highest pastures in the Andes, they were literally starving to death in the midst of their riches, because incurable diseases were wiping out their sheep and buffaloes.

Needless to say, they held the white lords responsible for their misfortunes, and, if the exaggerated slightly in claiming that their conquerors had visited their sorry fate upon them, they were not mistaken, in the sense that it was certainly the progress of civilization that had relegated them long ago to their remote mountains. However, according to a legend that had some authority among them, other white men would one day repair the injustice done to their ancestors, and two of them—one a superb old man full of wisdom—would come to the land of the Agzcéaziguls as saviors. The sick sheep and buffaloes would be cured, the livestock would multiply in a miraculous manner, wells would spring forth in the desert, crops would sprout amid the stones...in brief, there would be a new Golden Age and the end of the trial by ordeal of the Children of the Sun.

Georges Hiriburre had learned all that little by little, one scrap at a time, while patiently refraining from overly direct questions and avoiding seeming particularly interested, in order not to awaken the suspicions of the Indian chiefs who came to visit us—and you don't have to be a great scholar to figure out what seeds these revelations had sown in Georges' head.

It was very simple! We would go to find the Agzcé-aziguls in their domain, no matter how uncomfortable the journey was reputed to be, and we would announce to them that we were the liberators they were waiting for. After playing our comedy with all the desirable skill and audacity, it would only remain for us decamp quickly, without raising the alarm, with our pockets and pouches garnished with a quantity of gold and precious stones sufficient to permit us to live thereafter as princes on the banks of the Nive—or even somewhere else, if we chose.

Don't be indignant, honored sir; in France, or any nation properly ordered and policed, an act of that sort would, I grant you, qualify as mere theft, and even as theft with premeditation—but in the countries that were still new at the time of which I speak, it was simply Adventure. Adventure—especially when white men are only taking from red ones—in all its beauty, with its incalculable risks, but also with a fortune at its end, has the approval of everyone, and generates personal jubilation, when it is undertaken by a man who does not have cold in his eyes and knows how to prepare for it wisely!

IV

On November 10, 1858—which is to say, in spring-time, and in the most beautiful of spring-times—our material and other preparations were complete.

After much reflection and with no less meticulousness, Georges had traced the route that we would follow in red pencil on a large map. Our bales of provisions and clothes were strapped up, our water-bottles and weapons ready to be hitched on to our own backs or those of our mules. The mules had been brought to us the previous day in order that we might try them out—you can take my words for it that they were fine mounts! The merchant was supposed to come back a little later, the day after the next or thereabouts, to take his animals back if they had not pleased us, or to collect the price in the opposite case—but that was a detail that we did not recall until the evening of the following day, when we had already been en route since daybreak, and we burst into hearty laughter. It was not of the least importance; if we came back—and we certainly intended to do so—there would be every chance that we would easily be able to settle our account with the vendor, principal and interest. I'm making you laugh, now.

We still had to prepare, so that nothing was lacking and nothing was in excess, as delicately and as cleverly as possible, the accoutrements that we would have to don when we were not far distant from the land of our savages. In order not to give the lie to the legend, it was necessary that one of us should adopt the appearance of the redeemer-in-chief—the superb old man full of wisdom, remember? Georges had entrusted this role to me, estimating, with a good deal of common sense, that envoys of the gods would not have many words to say and that their appearance would be sufficient to establish them; to that end, I would be able to let him hold forth, since he could speak the native language perfectly.

For my part, though, I had many things to do. I had furnished myself with various items of disguise: an opulent white wig and a huge false beard, which, once adjusted, hung down to the level of my navel. I also brought along a rosary, which my poor grandmother had given me when I left Ustarritz—a big one, a meter long, with beads made of olive-stones from Carmel—whose cross I had replaced with a compass; by that means, the bounty of God and the science of men were united in a rare kind of talisman, to protect and aid us. That would complete my costume admirably when I hung it around my neck before I presented myself to the Agzcéazinguls. My costume? I must say that it was equal to the role. I had found it in a second-hand shop and had unhesitatingly paid outrageously dear for it, sure of not being able to find another that would have such a marvelous effect on our good Redskins: a purple silk robe sewn with gilt stars, which had once been used by a fairground charlatan. I must admit that, although the second-hand dealer made me pay ten times more than he had expected to get for that party-dress, he did throw in a pointed hat, matched as closely as he could, of dark blue velvet decorated with silver crescent moons.

We departed thus at daybreak, with no fanfare and all desirable discretion, but not without having honestly left the key in the door and sending the government a very dignified letter of resignation.

We followed the roads, and then the tracks, closest to the sea for some 50 Chilean leagues, and thus reached Huasco, where Georges decided to rest up for two days and three nights. It was there that we had to say goodbye, doubtless for a long time, to the civilized world—or what passed for such. After that, we headed north-east towards the mountains, proceeding in easy stages, in order to look after our mounts as best we could.

In the foothills of the Andes there was the marvelous festival of spring; myriads of minuscule jonquils and large blue or yellow irises were blooming alongside our scabrous paths, whose peppery and vanilla-flavored perfumes seemed to be distributed solely in our honor. Sometimes a condor circled around a few times at a scarcely respectable distance above our heads, and it was a pleasure for us—there being abundant ammunition in our bales—to teach it, by means of a well-directed bullet, that it was dealing with conquerors possessed of a wingspan at least the equal of its own. We were cheerful and confident. There was no lack of water; sweet and delightfully fresh, it fell into our mouths from the inaccessible and eternally snow-bound peaks that blocked the eastern horizon.

In brief, the journey promised to be a veritable pleasure trip. We only had to caress the hammers of our rifles one evening when three horsemen of a roguish appearance manifested an intention to borrow our mules and our baggage for a period whose duration they did not specify; sensing that we were ready to fire if they made the slightest movement towards the pistols in their belts, however, they turned around and galloped off to seek their fortune elsewhere, not without first telling us that there were no hard feelings on their part and asking us very politely to excuse them.

We left the lands frequented by white men shortly afterwards; we had nothing further to fear from them, and that was all to the good. We nevertheless experienced a slight apprehension when we came upon our first Indian encampment; we perceived them at a distance, on a vast plateau whose crossing would cut our route short.

"Let's not take any risks," I sad to my comrade. "I think it might be best to avoid these birds. There's a chance that a chief might recognize us."

Georges stopped, slapped his forehead and burst out laughing. "Good God, my old chap—without knowing it, you've suggested a good trick!"

A trick, in fact, that won us the most honorable and delightful welcome in that encampment and in all those that we encountered subsequently. Georges hastened to ask for the headman and, as soon as he found himself in his presence, announced to him with much ceremony that the government had sent us in order to carry out an enquiry on the subject of his just complaints—and as, ten times out of ten, the brave man had indeed, complaints that he was eager to make, he made every effort to obtain our friendship and esteem. Very often, in fact, we stumbled across old acquaintances, loyal clients of the Complaints Bureau, who fell to their knees before Georges, dazzled by so much solicitude.

There were feasts in our honor, dances and blow-outs. We even began to fall seriously behind the prearranged timetable. We were not in a hurry, to be sure, and our provisions were not exhausted, since we often found a good meal, good shelter and more on our road, but we had not gone there to amuse ourselves. Then again, it only required one slip-up on our part, and mistrust would spread like a gunpowder fuse from camp to camp and tribe to tribe, removing all hope of our reaching the land of the Agzcéaziguls and dying rich of old age.

"Enough larking about," I said to Georges Hiriburre, severely. "We have to be serious and focused now."

"Perhaps you're right."

Was it because we had been put to sleep by an excess of well-being? At that point in the journey everything suddenly changed, and the country was not conducive to restoring our good humor. Oh, the infinite extent of the desolate chain of the Sierra Grande, to which every step was bringing us nearer! We trotted for several days along its desert skirts, steering northwards along a dismal valley of which it seemed that we would never see the end. We no longer had anything to say to one another; we did not even have the heart to sing the good old silly songs of our homeland. We went forward at the behest of our mules, exhausted and depressed, as if the entire mass of the gigantic mountains that loomed up to our right were weighing down upon our shoulders and our souls.

The silence in this wilderness was prodigious, to the extent that the sound of a pebble rolling under the hoof of one of our animals or the raucous cry of a condor seemed veritably to fill the immensity of the sky...and we were overtaken by a confused and irrational anxiety, which we were forced to hide from one another and which neither of us dared admit to himself. One evening, in the dismal valley that had not yet come to an end, a violent storm gave us a glimpse of what the Last Judgment would be like, when the world ended.

The mules seemed insensible to our spurs that night. Our flight was more like a stampede. When dawn broke, Georges, whose courage had run out, began sobbing.

"I think we're lost. Suppose we make camp...and then turn back?"

"What's waiting for us in Santiago—or before then, on the road? Think about that!"

"Pooh! Working to death..."

I had to revive him by making him ashamed and feeding him brandy. Afterwards, he consented to consult his map and think hard.

"Yes, yes," he muttered, "I'm sure that we were too hasty. According to my calculations, we must, at this moment, be at the entrance to a gorge that the Indians call the Gate of Dawn. Do you see anything of that sort hereabouts?"

"In truth, no."

"There can't be any mistake, though; there can't be any other place on Earth that merits the name…"

"Why not?"

Georges became impatient. "You're becoming tiresome. What do I know? That's what it's necessary to understand. For one thing, the other Indian tribes hardly ever venture into this region, and their chiefs probably don't know it any better than we do. Damned savages! Filthy, stupid impostors! Tell me, Jean, were they making fun of us?"

"They wouldn't have done so deliberately. Don't get mad. Perhaps we came too far last night, as you said a moment ago…yes, in fleeing the storm. Come on—let's drink this bottle to the dregs."

Which we did.

That same day, slowly retracing our steps and passing very close to the first crags of the Sierra Grande—we had been going along the middle of the dismal valley until then—we encountered a sort of gigantic passage opening to our left. Do you know Roland's pass at Itxassou? Well, something of that sort. The river in the middle was only a stream thereabouts, but the cliffs on either side rose up at least 2000 feet.

We looked at one another, still uncertain, but he who risks nothing has nothing. We went into the passage, which was scarcely 300 meters wide, and as sonorous as an organ-pipe. The sunlight reflected so strongly from the gigantic walls of pink and yellow rocks that our eyes became useless, but when we closed them it was worse still, for all the colors of a demented rainbow danced painfully inside our eyelids.

Night came upon our eyes like a bandage on a wound. We profited from it to make further progress.

And then came the dawn.

We had stopped to let our animals breathe, and saw the Sun appear, as round as an eyeball, at the end of a straight and monstrous corridor which split, towards the east, like a half-closed eyelid...and the Sun rose, almost as if it existed that day for us alone. While its glare increased it seemed, by virtue of a curious optical phenomenon, not to be climbing into the sky but advancing along the passage to meet us.

Was this, therefore, the Gate of the Dawn? We had good reasons not to doubt it.

Then, the thought that we were near to our goal made us forget our weariness—and it was only a matter of rounding a rock on the bank to see the eye's opening, and the arrival of the good times.

V

To begin with, I took my priest-king's outfit from my bag: the beautiful gold-starred charlatan's cloak, the pointed hat with the silver moons, my rosary-and-compass, and the rest. When I was dressed, Georges held up a mirror for me—and truly, I had such a grandiose appearance in my white wig, with that immense prophet's beard, that I made a big impression on myself. If they did not immediately recognize me as the long-awaited liberator, our dear Agzcéaziguls would be very stupid—almost as stupid as that animal Georges, who wriggled in joy at the sight of me, clowning around extravagantly in my honor, finishing up by kneeling in front of me and intoning a Tyrolean yodel as a hymn to my glory—"Trou-lai-la-la..la..la..itou!!!"—so well that I thought it necessary to get sincerely angry, in order to shut him up.

"I'm well aware, old chap," I said to him, in response to his astonishment, "that I'm only your boss in pretence—but from now on, you have to conduct yourself as if it were the truth. You have to get into the habit—no gaffes, for God's sake, no gaffes! Otherwise, we'd be better employed making our wills than fine plans."

"I'm sorry, boss," bowing deeply, this time with the utmost seriousness. "If Your Lordship will take my advice though, let's stop for a moment to have a bite to eat and a little drink. At the same time, I'll have the honor of reading you something…"

He took a little notebook from his pocket, which I recognized; it was the one in which he had noted down all the information gathered at the Bureau of Indigenous Complaints.

"We have to go over our lesson," he said. Listen to what a headman in the Copiapo region told me a couple of months ago. It was the one we nicknamed Empty-Bottle, remember?"

"He rarely came without being drunk."

"Which loosened his tongue nicely. 'The Agzcéaziguls'—it's Empty-Bottle who's speaking—'are our beloved cousins, but we hardly ever see one another ; they rarely leave their encampments and hardly ever let other tribes in, even when beloved cousins go to pay them a little visit.' "

"Uh oh!"

"The beloved cousins are not liberators, nor Heaven-sent messengers," Georges told me, severely. "I continue: 'The Agzcéaziguls resemble us….' "

"Great! If their faces as are pretty as Empty-Bottle's…"

" '….resemble us. Their clothes and their bows are like those we use. Except, because of their great nobility, they have the right to attach golden bracelets furnished with small bells to their ankles, as the mountain chiefs used to do—and when they walk, you can hear the bells ringing…' "

"I've a good mind to stick the mules' bells on my legs," I said. "That'll bowl them over."

"Or annoy them," said Georges.

He riffled through the notebook again and beamed. "Listen—listen to what Empty-Bottle also said: 'One can't get into the land of the Agzcéaziguls easily…there's only one way in and it isn't easy to find....' Ah, Jean, cunning rogues that we are, we've found it all the same, that way in!"

"That's what we're about to find out. Hmm—the Sun's beginning to beat down. Mount up, comrade!"

"Will Your Grace permit me to hold his stirrup?"

While trotting on, we reflected on Empty-Bottle's statements and others of the same sort that Georges continued to read out from his little notebook. Suddenly, raising our heads, we saw an Indian mounted on a little grey horse a short distance away. We stopped. I lifted my eyes and my arms to the sky as if to call down all kinds of blessings upon him. After studying us in a bewildered and fearful manner however, he fled at a gallop and disappeared—not without our having had time to recognize the sound of little golden bells attached to his coarse leather gaiters.

"There's no mistake this time!" my companion cried, joyfully.

It was a stroke of luck for us to have encountered that brother. Otherwise, there was a chance that we might have turned back, with anger or discouragement in our hearts, persuaded that we had gone astray again. The Gate of the Dawn, you see, ended in an impasse formed by a semicircle of sheer rocks, even higher than the walls of the corridor!

We looked at one another dazedly. Unless we had gone mad, or had been victims of a hallucination, though, the existence of a way through had to be admitted. Otherwise, the Indian would have to have been phantom or to have possessed wings. We searched that tragic and desolate place desperately, rock by rock and stone by stone, but it was not until the evening that we discovered—purely by chance—a narrow crack opening obliquely in the rock, in front of which we might have passed ten times, but which was only visible from much further away, from a point situated at the center of the semicircle, and from nowhere else.

"Forwards! May God protect us!"

"Forwards! May God protect us!"

The cave was rapidly transformed into a sort of well-kept tunnel, with a smooth floor and polished walls, very wide and very straight, at the end of which a patch of fading daylight appeared. As we went forward night fell; the distant patch of light gradually vanished and was finally replaced by the luminous point of a star. Was that a good omen? It seemed so to us.

We pricked the flanks of our mules; as they broke into a trot again, the noise of their hooves echoed immensely.

We drew closer to one another. At the closest possible distance, Georges whispered in my ear: "Wait! Stop!"

"What's up?"

"Listen."

We heard the murmurous noise of a crowd: voices and footsteps which, in the subterranean gallery, reached us very distinctly.

"Damn," I said. "The brother that we met has advertised our arrival."

"And raised the alarm!"

"In any case, they're waiting for us at the exit. And it would be very annoying if these idiots, without asking us for explanations, prefer to strike us down as soon as we set foot on their territory."

"Let's go a little further—then I'll chance it."

We drew apart again, moderating our speed. When I was about 100 meters from the mouth of the tunnel, I halted my mount again. Georges did the same. Then, standing up in my stirrups, I made a little speech in Indian dialect—which Georges had prepared a long time before and I had learned by heart—in a resounding voice:

"Greetings, honor and glory to the noble Agzcéazigul people! I know of your undeserved sufferings, and my mission is to put an end to them. I am the old white man for whom you are waiting. My hands are peaceful and my designs breathe nothing but gentleness. I ask nothing from you but a little dry grass and water for our mules, and two places at your table for my servant and myself."

There was a silence that seemed to last for centuries, then a more ample ripple of murmurs and exclamations. Silhouettes of Agzcéazigul warriors stood out in black at the end of the tunnel against the livid pallor of the commencing night, like shadows on a badly-lit screen.

And still the silence, whose fragile edifice was finally broken by a single clear and sonorous voice: "If you are who you say you are, what are the evils from which we are suffering?"

Georges put his hand over my mouth, brutally. "Let me speak. That's my job—and don't forget that you, a priest and a king, restrict yourself in all circumstances to short speeches…"

Standing up in his stirrups in his turn, he shouted: "You are suffering from the injustice of my white brothers, from the poverty of the lands in which they have undeservingly imprisoned the sons of the Sun. Your herds are decimated by mysterious diseases. Those are the evil fates that have been visited upon you by the envious and the treacherous…but we know the spells that will set you free."

"Where do you come from?" said the voice at the end of the tunnel.

"From beyond the sea, and from even further away, The gods of our homeland spoke to us more than 20 Moons ago, and since then, we have been coming to you…"

"Can you give us proofs of what you say?"

I began to feel decidedly anxious, but Georges murmured, in a low voice: "Don't worry—I anticipated this." At the same time, after rummaging in his pockets, he pulled out an object that I could not make out at first, while replying to the anonymous inquisitor: "I can invoke your happiness and your present troubles, as best I can, O Children of the Sun, by courtesy of your illustrious ancestor, in transforming night into day at my whim."

And he lit a magnificent firework!

Immediately, a formidable acclamation resounded. Georges, mad with joy, thumped me twice in the ribs. "You see," he whispered, "that I have made my preparations well." And, a few minutes later, we emerged from the tunnel into the midst of 100 enthusiastic poor devils, who prostrated themselves before us in the dust, embraced our feet and our hands, and called us by the most flattering names that any mortal creature has ever heard.

Our dearest wish was to be allowed to sleep peacefully for a full 12 hours—but it was wise, to say the least, not to start with that.

After serious reflection as to what would stand the best chance of further raising my prestige, I got down from my mule, respectfully aided by my servant, and went to perch on a little mound. The good Indians formed a circle around me. Then I set about moving my head in every direction while shouting various Basque curses at the top of my voice, with a few Béarnais ones for good measure—in brief, performing the craziest routine I could think of…

All that took place amid a wonderstruck admiration and a religious silence. Suddenly, though, the sweat that was beading on my brow was succeeded by a cold sweat that ran all the way down my back. My wig was slipping and my beard was threatening to come undone. I hastened to affect the immobility of a fakir and to let George take over.

He immediately announced to the crowd that the gods appeared to me to be as well-disposed as possible, and that it was necessary to postpone the remainder of the ceremony to the next day, without importuning them further.

We were led to the largest and most beautiful tent in the neighboring encampment. A sumptuous feast was served to us there. We could not have asked for more from the gods whose temporary earthly representatives and guests we were.

Before going to sleep, we saw fires being lit in the mountains and heard the night-watchmen launching raucous cries from summit to summit, announcing the marvelous news of our arrival to the entire Agzcéazigul people.

VI

During the first week, my task consisted solely of blessing the herds that were brought to us from the four corners of
the territory. Prudently, Georges had put about the rumor that
the happy effects of my divine science would not be manifest
before the full Moon, which meant that we had two full weeks
in hand—and we hoped to be far away by the full Moon!

Many of our precautions were, however, superfluous for
the time being. Among the Agzcéazigüls, as among good
Christians, faith is the only route to salvation, and our hosts,
overwhelmed by gratitude, did not hesitate to proclaim that
their animals were much better already.

To be honest, I began to believe that it was true, and that
perhaps I possessed the gift of working miracles after all!

At other times, I experienced some remorse. As I explained to Georges—in the Basque language, as was only reasonable—I regretted not having recruited a veterinarian to our
expedition. For the same price you understand. It would have
been worthier and cleverer at the same time. We would have
had no need to hurry; we could have passed the time pleas-
antly for as long as we wished...

Georges shrugged his shoulders. "If the skinning disgusts
you, old man, best take a drink of Spanish wine. You're never
content, you old fool!"

I had no cause for complaint though. Kings visiting their
cousins are not treated as well as I was—to the extent that it
went to my head slightly...along with that wig, which made
me hot, and that damned beard, which threatened to come un-
stuck at any moment and sometimes put the wind up me.
Moreover, that was only the beginning of my glory! My companion, who always had his ear to the ground, told me that
something big was in preparation.

"It's a pity that you can't invite your old folks—what an
honor for the family that would be!"

Indeed, at the end of the first week, a cohort of about
1000 warriors appeared, greeted by the joyous cries of the

encampment, which had the fortunate distinction of having been the first to offer us hospitality. I learned that these brave men had come to take me, with great pomp, to Gunda, the holy city, in which the dead kings rested in the subterranean temples of the gods.

It was a pleasant journey, for whose entire length I was carried by a dozen men in a sumptuous litter, while poor Georges, slightly annoyed at being conclusively relegated to the rank of subaltern, jogged along by my side on one or other of our mules.

Gunda came in sight after 12ours of travel. What an astonishing and magnificent spectacle! Imagine, at the center of a prodigious circle of mountains, a combination of palaces of every form, classical or baroque, fabulous heaps of roseate stones, mingled with columns painted in garish colors—and, overlooking the holy city of Gunda, on the natural pedestal of a mountain, the gigantic statue of some god or devil, which stood out against the sky and whose upraised arms seemed to be supporting the weight of the setting Sun.

My cortège came to a halt at the summit of a narrow pass, at the idol's feet. The heralds that preceded us sounded their three-note horns and their ceremonial drums, for which the remains of buffaloes—horns and leather—had provided the materials centuries before, perhaps even in the time of the Incas. Songs reached my ears at the same time as the odor of meat grilling around hundreds of festival barbecues. Then another blast of horns and a new rumble of drums replied to us from afar, and the doors of one of the palaces on the plain were thrown wide open. I saw a host of horsemen spring forth in gala costume, bristling with feathers, brandishing bows, lances and maces, who rushed to meet us.

It was the guard of honor of the Agzcéazi guls' chief of chiefs, and the latter was galloping at the head of his most valiant warrior to put the insignia of supreme power in my hands!

Head lowered, heels together, stiff and humble, in the midst of a profound silence, the chief of chiefs handed me a hatchet, a bow, a dagger, a peace-pipe and various other objects whose significance and usage it is quite impossible for me to explain.

Thoroughly weighed down, I slipped the bow and the dagger and put the end of the peace-pipe between my lips. As to the other objects, having laid them out in front of me, I set about studying them in a pensive manner, while joining my hands—which appeared to complete the satisfaction of all the spectators, including the chief of chiefs. Intending to make a gesture of courtesy, I instructed Georges, still in the Basque language, to invite the latter to sit next to me in the litter; he refused obstinately, deeming himself unworthy of such an honor, but asked me as a favor whether he could ride the mule of which my servant had no need. I gave him permission gladly. He placed himself to my right, Georges remaining on my left, and the cortège set off again...

And that was the manner in which I arrived at the heart of the holy city of Gunda.

Then, jumping off the mule, the great chief went to stand before the door of the palace and, addressing himself by turns to me and his people, proclaimed: "This is my dwelling, Venerable One! Tell him, all of you, lest he doubt it! Do you hear? It is no longer me but him that all of you must serve! My warriors, my wealth and my power belong to you. I am no more than a dog at your feet. Never forget that, all of you!"

As for me, for want of anything better in his language, I launched once again into my initial speech: "Greetings, honor and glory to the noble Agzcéazigul people! I know of your undeserved sufferings, and my mission is to put an end to them..."

It was everlasting, that claptrap—as was proved when another tempest of enthusiasm gripped the crowd amassed around my litter. What? Would you believe, honored sir, that I might have returned to France as an ambassador such as has rarely been seen? But when one has been a king, you know, one has no desire for that sort of job. Golden bowls disdain mere dishes!

For I was a king—more than a king, almost a god! Immobile in my litter, I looked around, asking myself vaguely whether I might not be dreaming. Hordes of Indians were appearing at every moment at the end of every mountain path. The air vibrated with the loud acclamations that enfevered the pious silence one after another...

Well, would you believe me or not if I told you that suddenly, no longer merely dazzled but veritably astounded my glory, as if I were intoxicated, I eventually forgot the true reasons for my coming to Gunda, and persuaded myself that I really was, well and truly, the savior for whom these people had been waiting so long?

Alas, all that was no more than a grandiose comedy, which soon had to end.

VII

As soon as night fell, and we found ourselves alone in the depths of my royal dwelling, Georges took it upon himself to bring me back to a sense of reality. He did it rather cruelly—oh, I say that without any reproach...for he was right, entirely right, to do it!

"Well," he began, "it's probably best that we give some urgent thought to serious matters now."

"Do you think so? There's no hurry..."

"Damn it! You're beginning to get a taste for this existence!"

"Idiot!" I replied. "If I say that there's no hurry, it's because we have to act prudently."

"There's only one way that we can act prudently, and that's to be quick. Anything more is an unnecessary and dangerous luxury. At any moment, by virtue of the slightest little thing, our trickery might be discovered. And in this game, we're risking our hides, quite simply."

"I know that. As soon as the means present themselves, we'll choose from the riches accumulated around us the ones that are easiest to carry off, and *pfft!*"

"Right—that's the attitude."

The next day, after ostensibly spending several hours in meditation, I manifested the desire to go visit the tombs of the dead kings. The chief of chiefs deemed that to be a perfectly legitimate wish, which he granted with joyful piety. The annoying thing was that he thought it more appropriate and more honorable to have me escorted in this pilgrimage by a dozen his priests and dignitaries—but things were arranged to suit us when Georges explained to him that in our homeland, beyond the sea and more distant still, ceremonies of that sort were ordinarily conducted in the strictest privacy.

In the evening, it only remained for me to ask a sort of high chamberlain who had been put at my disposal to show me the way into the subterranean temples.

A funny chap, that chamberlain! I had only known him for a few hours, and had not had much to do with him, but he nevertheless inspired an instinctive mistrust in me. He was not at all like the others; the headman from the Copiapo district, good old Empty-Bottle had not lied to us when he said that the Agzcéaziguls resembled his subjects and himself—to tell the truth, between them and monkeys there was only a narrow margin—but the chamberlain, by contrast, was a well-built fellow, his face scarcely bronzed, lithe and alert...he'd have made a fine pelota player back home! There must have been a good deal of hybridization between our race and the South American races, I tell you, before the beautiful continent that served as the bridge between the two worlds was engulfed by the sea. Among us, you can see faces like his, with a pointed chin and prominent cheekbones, a hooked nose and slightly slanting eyes, all over the place, in blue berets and white trousers with a red belt, wandering around our villages of feast-days without attracting any attention at all.

With a funny look, he handed me a little gold lamp—the sacred lamp, he told me—and led me without further commentary to a little door, whose key he gave me. The door let out into a tunnel, at the end of which a spiral stairway descended abruptly into the ground.

Strongly suspecting that the sacred lamp would probably be insufficient, I had equipped myself, at the last moment, with a few candles, which had been wisely added to our luggage when it was packed.

Ninety steps, perhaps more…and I found myself in a colossal crypt, at the far end of which, on a sort of altar, 20 statues as large as big dolls were aligned. I picked one up, and shuddered. It was so very heavy! Solid gold, my honored sir, and furnished, in the form of eyes, with emeralds that must have been worth a fortune!

Here and there, in receptacles hollowed out in the very walls, little heaps of precious stones were sparkling. I took three or four handfuls very quickly, without being choosy, deploring the fact that I had never had the opportunity to become a connoisseur, and crammed them into a sheepskin bag that I wore around my neck between my shirt and my skin. Having filled the bag, I was already beginning to stuff my pockets, when I suddenly happened upon a chest full of ingots of pure gold…and, as that was a commodity more agreeable to me, I put the stones that were encumbering my pockets dutifully back where I had found them.

That crypt was succeeded by another after a long narrow corridor. I continued my stroll, weighed down by my booty, and also slightly disturbed by the funereal silence. Then my disquiet was transformed into a fever—a veritable fever, whose pulse I felt in my wrists and temples, so powerfully that it seemed to me that the tunnel must be reverberating with its beat…

I had arrived at a place where the stone coffins of defunct chiefs were lined up as far as the eye could see, far beyond the limit of the shadows. It seemed to me then that I was no longer alone, that a phantom had just passed in front of me, in the region that the rays of my luminary did not reach…

The idea of the sacrilege that I was committing filled me then, for several seconds, with dark presentiments...

Suddenly, resolved to see no more on this occasion, I turned around—and found myself face to face with the chamberlain!

I felt better—but I had just experienced a violent emotion! While I hastened to collect myself, the imprecations that the Indian was jabbering clearly demonstrated to me that he had foreseen everything, understood everything, seen everything...and that our plans were discovered.

There could be no more hesitation; there was no time. I slid my hand to my belt and, with a single well-aimed pistol-shot, sent the foolhardy individual rolling at my feet, choking and vomiting blood.

By the time I had prudently reloaded my weapon, he was dead.

I went back to Georges and told him what had happened. He listened anxiously, without interrupting me, his forehead furrowed by a deep and anxious wrinkle. When I had finished, he simply said: "Show me your harvest. That little bag of stones and a few gold ingots? Damn! It's a poor crop—it's hardly worth the trouble, especially with the surfeit of danger that the stupid incident will store up for us."

"What do you want?" I said to him. "Now that the man is dead, we can't do anything but flee immediately—or before dawn, at any rate..."

"What rotten luck! A unique opportunity. Oh...but I haven't said my last word yet. So much gold! Golden statues!" After a brief and pregnant silence, with his eyes sparkling with avarice, he went on, in a hoarse and tremulous voice that I had never heard before: "Tell me, Jean, the statues on the altar...how big are they? How heavy?"

"Too big, too heavy...it would be madness to load ourselves down with them."

He hesitated, then, with his fists clenched, tapping his foot on the ground, he said: "That's a pity. Let's go and get one, at least."

At the thought of going back into that vast and dismal underworld, where the cadaver of my victim now lay, I could not help shivering.

"It's insane...insane..." I stammered, feebly.

Georges looked at me in a rather scornful manner, which hurt my heart, then shrugged his shoulders and replied: "I understand. I don't want you to...it's all right, I'll go alone. Fetch our mules, or horses if you can't get them..." Then he had second thoughts. "No, I'll go very quickly. In the state you're in, you don't inspire me with confidence. Don't budge—wait for me."

When he reappeared after half an hour, exhausted and bathed in sweat, he was carrying—or, rather, dragging—four massive gold idols, tied together...and not the least of them, I assure you!

"Well," he exclaimed, triumphantly, "What do you say?"

"It's too much...too much!"

"Isn't it what you need to be a king everywhere, or at least to put on a good show...other than among savages?"

I made no reply. Overcome by a bleak despair that George might have taken for perfect calmness, I set about packing up the statues while he went in search of our mounts. It seemed to me that he took a long time to come back; dark thoughts seethed within my head. I had to empty a big bowl of rice brandy—a gift from our hosts—at a single draught. As soon as he returned, though, Georges reassured me: "Everything's going to plan."

"Our mules?"

"They're waiting placidly in front of your palace."

"And my...subjects?"

"They're fast asleep, wearied by feasting and the libations they've drunk in your honor."

There was better news. He had gone up to the top of a tower that flanked our dwelling and, from the height of that observatory, had noticed that the innumerable tents of the Ag-zcéaziguls were only erected on one side of the plain; we would have the road that led to the Gate of the Dawn at our disposal. Finally, the entire nation being gathered at Gunda, there was reason to believe that we would not meet anyone unexpectedly on the way, and that our retreat would be effected through a veritable desert.

"What about the sentinel?" I asked, suddenly. "The one standing guard outside our door?"

"Oh, don't worry. He doesn't suspect anything. He's sleep, sound asleep. He won't wake up!"

"What do you mean?"

He contented himself with sniggering ferociously; then, having shown me that he no longer had more than one dagger in his belt, he put a finger upon his heart and said: "I left the other one there, fully embedded. Neat work, I assure you!"

Oh well! I swear to you—I, who had felt horror in the marrow of my bones an hour before, the glacial effect of a crime that I had been fully obliged to commit—that on learning of that one, whose necessity I could not see at all, I experienced not the slightest pang of emotion…nothing at all! And, as my companion had begun sniggering again, I began to laugh too—an interminable and stupid laughter!

In truth, we were drunk: drunk on blood and gold, blood that we had both shed, drunk on that savage and hard gold whose vertiginous possessions was driving us mad!

VIII

Sober men are apt to say that there is a God who looks after drunkards; our particular intoxication certainly appeared to merit his attention just then. Our departure passed unnoticed; within a quarter of an hour we had left the tents far behind us to our right. In brief, everything happened as Georges, in his optimism, had anticipated a few minutes earlier.

Our mules, valiant beasts that they were, maintained a speedy trot even though they were loaded down by our marvelous burden, and while we drew further away, without any thought of sleep or any desire to eat or drink, we devoted ourselves joyfully to planning crazy future projects, feeling stronger and more powerful than if we had been masters of the world....

The intoxicating effects of gold are essentially similar to those of wine. Our exaltation was succeeded by an immense lassitude, an irresistible desire to sleep at all costs. As it seemed to us that half an hour's siesta would be enough to set us straight, Georges swore to me that he would not close an eye until he had woken me up. Less than ten minutes later, alas, we were snoring as loudly as one another.

When we open our eyes, we observed, fearfully, that the night was already about to end. A tragic light was already bloodying the eternal snows in the east. Georges struck his breast and tore his hair despairingly. It was even worse when we perceived fires being lit in various places beneath us, on the plain that we had already left before our ill-timed nap, regularly spaced and seemingly ominous. There was no doubt that, the alarm having been sounded, all the Agzcéazigul people would launch themselves in pursuit in a few minutes' time.

"It's my fault, my fault!" Georges groaned. "And I should have hidden the sentinel's corpse!"

"What's done is done. Quickly—mount up!"

Abruptly sobered up, without pity for our overloaded mules, still worn out with fatigue, we whipped them unmercifully. There followed a desperate flight through the half-light, which was vague and deceptive at that hour, gong straight ahead, somewhat at hazard.

Shortly after daybreak, we had just paused to let our animals catch their breath when a blast of horns resounded close by.

"There they are!" Georges murmured, going very pale. "We're done for!"

At present, I firmly believe that the people giving chase to us ought not and could no have been at our heels yet, however intense their indignation and thirst for vengeance might have been. In those mountain regions, the complicated play of echoes often produces veritable sonic mirages, and it is probable that we had been cruelly deceived by a phenomenon of that sort—as you can imagine, though, we did not take the time to reflect on all that!

Again, the flight became desperate. We went up and down the steepest slopes, scornful of bone-breaking falls, risking everything to gain everything, sending fragments of rock flying and raising eddies of dust behind us.

It was only after two hours of that demented gallop that I noticed that we were on a path that was completely unfamiliar, leaving the Gate of the Dawn to our right.

In the far distance, however, almost at the limit of the horizon, beyond the declining undulations of the Sierras, the sea appeared in the bright light of a fine day, as if at the foot of a gigantic stairway, on the highest step of which we still remained.

The sea! Salvation! Down there, the Agzcéazioguls would not be able to find us; down there we would be able to obtain security for our wealth and ourselves, and begin to enjoy the fruit of our efforts—not to mention cultivating our hopes in peace. Then we galloped again, no longer like hunted beasts but like prisoners who feel new strength born within them as they approach the frontier at which the authority of their persecutors expires.

We raced from heights into ravines, and from valleys to summits, having only one desire and one idea lodged in our heads: to see the sea again, after having lost it in the depressions of the terrain. It was as if our eyes were thirsty for it! We devoured the distance, careless of the frightful paths we took, animated by the sole desire to go by the shortest route, forgetting the precipices to which our mules' hooves sometimes came exceedingly close.

Dusk fell. I had been leading the way for some time. Almost sure that we were nearly out of reach—the Agzcéaziguls, courageous in their own domain, must have abandoned the chase, sick at heart—I was about to talk about getting a little rest and nourishment when a frightful cry of rage and distress resounded from behind me.

Georges' mule, its strength exhausted, had suddenly collapsed—and, dragging its rider with it, had fallen into the depths of an abyss.

Leaping to the ground, I went forward, still in doubt, convinced that I was the victim of some atrocious illusion, repeating: "It's a trick, a dirty trick. Georges! Enough! Come on! Don't make the animal...it's no good!" And I laughed...laughter that frightened me, and which seemed to sting my throat.

At the very bottom, more than 100 meters below me, the man and the beast were lying inert. Lying face down, stretched out full length on the lip of the chasm, directly above them, dazed by horror and vertigo, I contemplated that horrible spectacle for a long time with demented eyes...and I noticed—yes, even today, I'm sure that I wasn't mistaken, that I really saw it—I noticed that poor Georges' head, around which a large halo of blood had already spread, scarlet against the ocher ground, was obscured, flattened and broken by one of the golden statues that had fallen on top of it...on top of it, you understand, not beside it.

You'll tell me, honored sir, that there was nothing in that but a scarcely extraordinary matter of chance, and I'll agree with you. At the time, though, racked by emotion and fatigue, trembling on the edge of delirium and madness, I saw it as manifest proof of the vengeance of the offended Agzcéazigul gods. Fear, you see, can take a man back hundreds of thousands of years from his own time, to the bestiality and naivety of his remotest ancestors. Well, that evening, I pleaded for the clemency of idols like a savage: I, who, too young and perhaps too soon—assuming that there is ever an age to do it—had already forgotten to pray to the Virgin and the Saints!

Yes, detaching from my saddle the two statues of which I had taken charge, I remember taking them religiously, with trembling hands, to install them in a hollow in the rock, then kneeling down in front of them, sobbing, and begging them, in their own language—reasonably competently—to spare me: "Abrezaïrig…! Abrezaïrig…!" Which means, to be best of my recollection: "Pardon me!" or even "Have pity on me!"

And in the rays of the Sun, which was setting almost directly facing the idols, it seemed to me that I saw the emeralds that served them as eyes light up, roll and move between their golden eyelids….

"Abrezaïrig…! Abrezaïrig…!"

That lasted until the moment when, the excess of terror having given me a little strength, I succeeded in turning my head, in detaching my living eyes from their bewitched eyes. It was as if an evil spell had been broken momentarily, as might happen to a man condemned to death whose keepers lose sight of him for a second…

And, leaving my mule there, without even a last glance at my poor comrade, I resumed my flight, with empty hands and a brain on fire…

Empty hands. Yes, I had left the two idols there. They're probably there still.

I can assure you that would rather have continued my journey holding a bowlful of the embers of Hell in my hands.

IX

My story ends there…there, in truth, honored sir. How I reached the edge of the sea, I cannot remember myself, and cannot tell you. There is every reason to believe that I was quite mad for several whole days, while I followed my route on foot; whether I slept, ate or drank during that time, I don't know. It was a party of horse-traders on their way from Chanaral to Caldera along the cliff path who picked me up and cared for me.

I learned a few days later, when I had partly recovered my senses, that they had fond me capering and gesticulating on the beach at the foot of the cliff, hurling pebbles into the sea and swearing that the pebbles were ingots of gold—a bewitched and accursed gold that was weighing my pockets down frightfully. At the time when I learned this detail, my pockets were, indeed, full of pebbles...

For a moment, I wondered whether my saviors had taken advantage of my delirium to rob me...but I was already lucid enough not to waste much time on that idea; if the horse-traders really had robbed me, they would undoubtedly have killed me there and then—which would, from the viewpoint of their narrow interests, have rounded off the affair neatly.

In retrospect, after many years and fully burdened by experience, I suppose that I had gathered the pebbles that filled my pockets on the beach, after throwing the ingots of solid gold stolen from the Agzcéazigul chiefs—which would have been enough to make a man rich, and great in the eyes of the world, for the rest of his days—into the sea...

Nowadays, I live on cheap wine and crab soup, with a bit of rancid bacon on Sundays, ten *sous*' worth of meat for feast-days, and fruits when I find them hanging outside the orchard walls...but I've never regretted the things I did during those hours of madness, never grieved for that accursed gold, for which my beloved Georges Hiriburre had to die, his bones broken and his skull smashed, at the bottom of a chasm in the Sierra Grande. Would I, who enjoy a fundamental peace and happiness, rather have shared his fate, serving as a meal for the vultures of the Andes? I'm perfectly certain, honored sir, that I would not.

Afterwards, I went globe-trotting again, all over the world. I probably saw worse and stranger things...the sirens of

Cape Horn...the Ship of the Dead [5]...the City of Monkeys...
All of that is heaped up in my memory, slowly diminishing in importance as my back becomes bent and I shrivel up myself. That shriveling works to my advantage, in diminishing the cruelty of the memory, for I sometimes succeed in imagining that my journey with Georges to the land of the Agzcéaziguls might, perhaps, have happened in a dream, after all...except that...

Jean Aruégoyen pauses for a long time, then slips a hand into his woolen cardigan and takes out a little sheepskin bag.

"Except that...I still have this to prove that I didn't dream it..."

Then, on the shabby table in the little inn, he turns the bag over, and releases a flood of precious stones: emeralds, sapphires, topazes, beryls, aquamarines, chrysoprases and chrysoliths...and then he looks down at them, bleakly, while you exclaim:

"But in that case, Jean...your pretended poverty...the cheap wine...the crab soup...?"

Calmly, he puts the stones in the sheepskin bag, and the sheepskin bag between his cardigan and his skin...

"Fakes, monsieur...as they did not hesitate to tell me when I wanted to sell a few of them, when I was starving yet again. Fakes, clever fakes. Oh, honored sir, the crab soup, the cheap wine and the memories of ancient disappointments are nothing, but what will vex me until my final hour—for there is no other possible explanation of the presence of those shoddy goods in the tomb of a chief of the Children of the Sun—is the idea that people of our sort must have caught wind of the story

---

[5] Jean's encounter with the legendary Ship of the Dead is related in "*L'épave tragique*" [The Tragic Wreck], another story included in the collection for which "*Les conquérants d'idoles*" serves as the title-piece, but I do not know whether Derennes recorded the other adventures recalled in this passage.

before Georges and I did, that we were preceded in the holy city of Gunda, that they must surely have anticipated the slightest details of such an adventure better than we did...and that they must have obtained—everything supports this conclusion—infinitely more profit than we did.

THE END